W9-CFN-770

"He's following us."

Abigail's face had gone deathly pale, and she clutched her son closer.

Micah whipped his head around. The man she'd pointed out a few minutes ago had picked up his pace and was now heading straight toward them. His brown hair and stature were about right for the man who'd fled Abigail's home.

Micah pressed a hand against Abigail's back and guided her in front of him toward the doorway to the next room. More tourists had piled into the place in the past fifteen minutes, maybe even a tour bus or two judging by the crowd. Could they lose the man in here?

Abigail ducked off to the side, partially shielding herself from view behind a tall spinning rack of mini South Dakota license plates. "We have to split up. It's me they're after. You take Owen to my sister, and I'll lead him away."

She pressed her lips to her son's hair, then shoved him into Micah's arms. "Wait, Abigail, it's too—"

Dangerous. The word died on his tongue as she walked away from him.

Kellie VanHorn is an award-winning author of inspirational romance and romantic suspense. She has college degrees in biology and nautical archaeology, but her sense of adventure is most satisfied by a great story. When not writing, Kellie can be found homeschooling her four children, camping, baking and gardening. She lives with her family in western Michigan.

Books by Kellie VanHorn

Love Inspired Suspense

Fatal Flashback
Buried Evidence
Hunted in the Wilderness
Dangerous Desert Abduction

Visit the Author Profile page at LoveInspired.com.

DANGEROUS DESERT ABDUCTION

KELLIE VANHORN

LOVE INSPIRED SUSPENSE

INSPIRATIONAL ROMANCE

If you purchased this book without a cover you should be aware that this book is stolen property. It was reported as "unsold and destroyed" to the publisher, and neither the author nor the publisher has received any payment for this "stripped book."

LOVE INSPIRED® SUSPENSE

INSPIRATIONAL ROMANCE

Recycling programs
for this product may
not exist in your area.

ISBN-13: 978-1-335-59898-1

Dangerous Desert Abduction

Copyright © 2023 by Kellie VanHorn

All rights reserved. No part of this book may be used or reproduced in any manner whatsoever without written permission except in the case of brief quotations embodied in critical articles and reviews.

This is a work of fiction. Names, characters, places and incidents are either the product of the author's imagination or are used fictitiously. Any resemblance to actual persons, living or dead, businesses, companies, events or locales is entirely coincidental.

For questions and comments about the quality of this book, please contact us at CustomerService@Harlequin.com.

Love Inspired
22 Adelaide St. West, 41st Floor
Toronto, Ontario M5H 4E3, Canada
www.LoveInspired.com

Printed in U.S.A.

Behold, what manner of love the Father hath bestowed upon us, that we should be called the sons of God.
—*1 John* 3:1

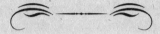

For my brother Matt, who always makes me laugh.

With endless thanks to Kerry Johnson,
Michelle Keener, Ali Herring, and
editors Katie Gowrie, Shana Asaro and Dina Davis,
along with the rest of the Harlequin Love Inspired team.
I couldn't do this without you!

ONE

Abigail Fox glanced over her shoulder as she pushed the shopping cart out of the store. No sign of the man with the red ball cap who'd been watching her at the checkout. Maybe she'd only imagined he was following her.

She picked up her pace anyway. The parking lot had grown dark while she shopped, and a shiver tracked its way down her back as she headed toward her SUV. Most of the shoppers had cleared out, leaving her vehicle forlorn and alone in a dark section of the lot. She should've paid more attention to the locations of the lights in the lot when she'd parked the car.

She steered around a pothole in the pavement, careful not to wake her four-year-old son, Owen. He'd fallen asleep in the cart as she gathered the items they'd need over the next few days. His little blond head lay propped up on a jacket and her handbag, his long lashes fanning plump cheeks. Hopefully he'd stay asleep until they made it to their tiny rental outside Badlands National Park. She'd picked up the key this afternoon, intending to unload the trunk at that time, but the place had looked so desolate that she couldn't bring herself to get out of the car. Instead, they'd driven another hour to Rapid City to pick up groceries.

Now with the sun gone and night blanketing the parking lot, she was second-guessing that decision.

But surely no one would look for them out here. She'd driven two days from Chicago. Nine hundred miles lay between them and Eric's killers. There was no way those men could've followed her—was there?

A wave of exhaustion slammed into her and she leaned against the cart as it rattled over the pavement. Her vision clouded. Things shouldn't have to be this hard, not if God truly cared about her personally. Maybe things hadn't been great in their marriage, but they'd been a family, she and Eric and Owen.

She gazed at Owen's sweet, sleeping form, his thumb sliding out of his mouth as she rolled the cart to a stop behind her vehicle. She could do this for him. She *had* to, no matter how terrified and alone she felt. They'd get through this together. She dug out her keys, unlocked the car and popped the trunk. There wasn't much space—she had to stuff the bags of groceries between the duffels and boxes waiting to be unloaded. All their important worldly belongings.

As she worked, she glanced up at the glowing storefront. A few other shoppers trickled out, heading for their vehicles, but no one seemed to be paying attention to her. *Good.* But then why was the hair on her arms standing on end?

A car pulled up in front of the store, off to one side, and a passenger climbed in. She forced her eyes back to the cart and wedged the last few bags into the packed trunk, cramming them securely into place before closing the hatchback. Headlights suddenly illuminated her like she was on a theater stage, and she stepped between the vehicle and Owen to shield him from the brightness.

She shivered as the car coasted past then pulled into a spot one over from her SUV. What possible reason could the driver have for parking way out here? As she turned the shopping cart around, the vehicle's lights cut out and the driver's door opened, the engine idling.

She nearly jumped out of her skin when

the driver stepped out and called her name. "Abigail! Abby, is that you?"

Wait, she recognized that voice. Frowning, she pivoted slowly. "David? What are you doing here?" One of Eric's accounting friends, he'd become a regular visitor in their home for meals and board games over their years in Chicago. He'd been incredibly helpful in the past three weeks since the funeral, offering financial guidance, helping sort Eric's things, entertaining Owen when she needed a minute.

But why was he *here*? She hadn't shared the full scope of the police investigation after Eric's death. David only knew what everyone had heard—that a month ago Eric had gone into the office where he worked as a CPA and shot himself at his desk. She hadn't told anyone—not even her sister or parents—that the police suspected her husband had gotten tangled up in organized crime. According to the evidence, Eric had wiped his hard drive and shredded all his client files before killing himself. Like he had something to hide and couldn't take the guilt—a story confirmed by a two-line suicide note that didn't match his handwriting, at least to her eyes. But Officer Bernetto, the man in charge of the case, had merely noted her concerns and said he'd "look into it."

Eric may have had his faults, but he wouldn't have taken his own life. No, it made far more sense he'd crossed the wrong person, especially with the way he'd grown increasingly secretive and stressed over the past several months. The overtime at work, the phone calls at odd hours, the strangers dropping off envelopes...

"Thank goodness," David said as he strode closer. "I haven't been able to sleep since we talked the other night." He'd called to check on her the first night she and Owen were on the road. Overwhelmed and alone in a Wisconsin hotel, she'd wanted *someone* to know where they were going, so she'd shared her Google Maps route with him and her sister. For Owen's sake, just in case anything happened.

"I know you told me you're fine," he went on, "but after the break-in last week, I've been worried about you. I had some time off and wanted to make sure you were okay."

The break-in at her house had been all over the news—rare in her bungalow belt neighborhood—so it wasn't surprising he'd be concerned. Someone had torn the place up but not taken anything, like they couldn't find what they wanted. More evidence Eric had been involved in something big.

"You drove all the way out here? I appreciate the thought, but you could've just texted or called." Maybe she shouldn't have told him where she was going.

He edged closer, one hand out. "I had to see for myself you were both okay. It's been a rough month."

She inched closer to the cart. Something felt off about him chasing after her, like sandpaper chafing at a tender patch of skin. "Did you tell anyone you were coming to find me? Where you were going?"

His thick blond eyebrows pulled together. "No, but why would it matter? Abby, is there something going on you haven't told me about? Are you in trouble?" His voice softened, and he extended a hand. "Do you need help?"

She chewed her lip. For a split second, she imagined spilling the whole story. Letting him step in and take charge. How good it would feel not to bear this burden alone. That officer who'd handled her case in Chicago had only made things worse, pressuring her to find anything Eric might have left behind that could be tied to criminal activity. Then the break-in had happened. The letter from Eric written the day of his death but delayed in the mail. The threatening man who'd turned up on her doorstep demanding "the files."

That very night, she'd packed up Owen and their things and hit the road.

But if she told David, she'd be putting him in danger too, wouldn't she?

And the fact he'd driven out here after her... Maybe it *should* feel like a grand gesture, but somehow it seemed all wrong. Like he hadn't listened to what she'd said or respected her decisions. Even the way he'd taken to calling her "Abby" lately instead of her full name grated on her.

She tightened her grip on the shopping cart. "No, I'm fine. You shouldn't have come all the way out here. We just wanted to take a trip and get out of the city."

David's gaze hardened, and her pulse kicked up. He'd never looked at her that way before. When he shifted his weight, flicking one hand near his side like a signal, her breath caught.

"You're not really the traveling type, Abigail." The words came out low and menacing.

Behind him, the passenger door opened, and someone stepped out.

The man with the red ball cap and black

shirt from inside the store. Her stomach dropped. He *had* been following her.

"Who's that?" She licked her too-dry lips. "What's going on?"

"Doesn't matter. What does matter is that Eric was in deep with the wrong people. They know he kept records that could be used against them. They know about the letter, and—"

"How?" she interrupted. She'd shown that to no one except the police. Eric had written it the day of his death, but his office mailroom had lost it until last week. And unlike the suicide note, she had no doubt he'd written this one. Mostly it had been an apology, except for Eric's mention of a safe deposit box—one Abigail knew nothing about. Officer Bernetto had concluded that Eric must have important documents hidden in it and pressured her to find it. But you couldn't squeeze blood out of a turnip, as the saying went. No amount of pressure was going to make her suddenly understand what Eric's letter meant.

Had he shown it to David before he mailed it? Or someone else?

"Doesn't matter," David said. "What does matter is that they know you went to the bank three days ago just before skipping town. Did you get the files? Is that why you ran?"

Those files again! The same thing the man on her doorstep had demanded.

"No," she shot back. "I withdrew cash to use while we were traveling. I have no idea about any files!" He *had* to believe her—it was the truth. She glanced around the lot, hoping someone else might see or intervene. Should she scream, or would it be too risky with the other man nearly beside her?

David's lips pressed together, and he shook his head. "Not good enough, Abby." He nodded toward her car. "Are they in the car? I can wait while you pull them out."

"No, I don't—"

He closed in, clapping his hand over her mouth, and Abigail flinched. The other man was behind her in a flash, pinning her arms to her side. Dragging her backward, away from Owen, away from the storefront where others might see what was happening, and out of view behind the cover of her SUV.

"Here's the thing." David leaned in so close his breath burned her cheek. "I can't protect you and Owen any longer. I warned Eric this would happen, and he didn't listen. You get this one last chance because we were friends."

Fear tightened her throat, threatening to choke her. Owen shifted in the cart, settling deeper against her jacket. So innocent, utterly unaware of the world crashing down around them.

Across the parking lot, footsteps thudded on asphalt and a male voice rang out. "Hey, what's going on?"

David shot a glance at the man holding Abigail and yanked his hand away. She screamed, but the sound was instantly muffled by the other man's hand. David rushed at the cart, tugging Owen out as the world shifted beneath Abigail's feet.

No no no.

Not her son. *Please, God, not Owen!*

She writhed and kicked against the man's grasp, but his arms were like steel as David slid into the back seat of the car with Owen, whose eyes were still shut in the bliss of slumber. "You've got until tomorrow morning, Abby. Until then, I'll keep him safe. You have my word. But you better get those files," David said. Then, "Vincenzo, now!"

The back door slammed shut.

"Let her go!" the other voice commanded. Footsteps pounded to a halt a few feet away and a man emerged around the back of the SUV. His long, dark hair was swept to one side, and a short beard covered his jaw. But nothing could hide the concern and anger reflecting in his bright blue eyes.

"If you want to see the kid again, you better come up with those files," Vincenzo snarled, then abruptly shoved her toward the man.

Abigail stumbled forward. She would've gone down entirely if the man hadn't caught her, his hands wrapping around her waist just long enough for her to find her footing.

Behind her, the car door slammed shut, the headlights kicked on and the sedan drove off.

With Owen.

The woman stood with her back to Micah Ellis, hands pressed to her face, her entire body trembling as the car roared out of the parking lot. Talk about providential timing. He'd stayed late to help clean up after the evening church service, and then this last-minute run to the grocery store. The quick detour had landed him in the parking lot right when he was needed. *Thank You, God.*

"Are you all right?" He reached for her shoulder but stopped shy of touching her.

A sob burst from behind her hands and she pivoted around, turning wide green eyes on him. "Owen," she gasped. "They took Owen. My son."

Micah's stomach dropped. He'd seen someone climb into the backseat, heard the door slam, but he hadn't realized they'd taken her child—

No wonder she looked so frantic.

"I'm Micah Ellis, law enforcement ranger at Badlands National Park." Not that he looked like a ranger right now, out of uniform in his khakis and a button-down. He dug into his pocket, pulling out his badge and cell phone. After flashing her the badge, he tapped in the number for the Rapid City PD but waited to initiate the call. "I'm going to help you, but I need a little more information. What's your name?"

She turned to him, eyes unfocused, and swayed slightly. He shot out an arm to steady her, then gently guided her to the rear of her SUV. She collapsed onto the bumper with a soft sob. His gaze caught on the license plate—Illinois. She wasn't from around here. Maybe that explained the dark circles under her eyes, and the way her auburn hair was slipping out of its bun in thick clumps around her wan cheeks. Her clothing, a plain blue T-shirt and pair of loose green slacks, looked high end but considerably rumpled. Had she just arrived in this part of the state?

"What?" she murmured, like she hadn't heard him.

He dropped down to her eye level and

locked his gaze on hers. "We're going to help Owen, but I need more information, and I need it fast. What's your name?"

She shook her head, like she was clearing out the cobwebs, and straightened. "Abigail Fox."

"And can you describe Owen for me?"

"Blond hair, brown eyes." Her expression softened, like she was losing focus. "He looks just like Eric."

Not an observation that would help. Who was Eric? Her husband? Yet her left ring finger was empty—newly so, judging by the thin band of pale skin. "How old is he?"

"He just turned four. A few days after the funeral." She pressed a hand to her heart, and his insides twisted, but he kept his mind focused on the details.

"So maybe three feet, forty pounds?"

As she nodded, he clicked the green "call" button on his phone. It was late, after regular work hours, so he was surprised when his friend, Detective Brian Overton, answered rather than a night officer.

"Brian, it's Micah. What are you doing working the desk this late?"

"Hazel has an ear infection and nobody can sleep, so Jules told me I might as well catch up on some cases." He yawned, as if to punctuate his words. "I volunteered to cover the front for a couple of minutes."

"Sorry about the baby," Micah offered. Hazel was Brian and Julie's first, born earlier that year in January. "I hate to lay this on you, but I'm in the Rapid City supermarket parking lot and we need an Amber Alert."

Abigail pressed her hand to her mouth as he spoke, relaying the details to his friend. "Four-door sedan. I think it was a Lincoln Town Car, dark blue or black. I didn't get the plates."

"I know who took him," she interrupted.

Who? Micah mouthed. Then into the phone, he said, "Hold on a sec, there's more."

"David Blakely, from Chicago. There was the other man too, the one with the red ball cap, but I don't know him. His name is Vincenzo."

Micah nodded, then passed the information on to Brian. After he ended the call, he turned to her.

"That's enough to issue the Amber Alert. He wants us to come down to the precinct so he can get more information from you."

She nodded, her gaze blank as he pointed at his blue sedan farther up the lot. "That's my car. Are you okay to drive? Can you follow me?"

His cell phone buzzed at the same second hers did from inside the leather handbag in the nearby shopping cart. She rushed for it, digging it out, then clutched the cart to keep her balance.

He glanced down at the notification.

Amber Alert: Rapid City area.

Good. Hopefully someone would see the car and get back to the police within minutes.

The city streets were mostly empty as he led Abigail to the police department. The front desk officer, who had returned, directed the two of them to Brian's cubicle in the detectives' office.

Brian shook his hand and offered Abigail a seat and a steaming cup of coffee. It didn't take long to go over what had happened. She sat still as a statue through the conversation, the only motion the soft rubbing of her fingers. Particularly, the empty ring finger on her left hand.

"Is there any more information you can give us?" Brian asked. "Any reason why David might have wanted to take Owen?"

She drew in a shuddering breath, and Micah leaned forward, propping his elbows on his knees. Maybe now he'd learn why she was here in South Dakota.

"My husband died four weeks ago," she murmured. Her shoulders curled and she stared at her hands. That explained the pale band around her finger instead of a ring. Poor woman—newly widowed, and now her son taken. He grimaced. Wasn't that the way relationships always ended? In heartbreak?

He and Brian listened as she poured out her story, sharing how her accountant husband appeared to have taken his own life—though *she* thought he'd been killed—and the police suspicions he'd been involved with an organized crime syndicate, maybe even the Chicago Outfit. The mafia was no laughing matter. She seemed to grow smaller with each passing minute, sinking deeper inside herself.

"What about this man, David Blakely? How is he involved?" Brian asked.

"He's a family friend. Owen calls him 'Uncle' David." A shiver rippled through her shoulders. "He and Eric studied accounting together in business school, though they worked for different companies. He must be connected with this crime group somehow." She sucked on her upper lip. "I had no idea." Her voice dropped out.

Anger flared in Micah's chest at the mess

this unknown husband had created for his wife. But he needed to focus on the most pressing matter—getting Owen back. "Why would David want Owen? Did he say anything to you?"

She nodded, sniffling softly, and Brian handed her a tissue. "Eric mailed me a letter the morning he died. The mailroom lost it, so it just arrived last week. He apologized, told me I had the chance to make things right. He said he'd made me the trustee of a safe deposit box. All I can think is that it must contain evidence the police could use against the ringleaders of the mob, and somehow the mob figured it out too. They think I already found the files when I went to the bank to get cash before Owen and I left, but I don't even know where this box is."

She pressed a hand to her mouth as she shook her head. "Eric never mentioned it to me before, and the letter doesn't say. I checked every bank we've ever had accounts with." She turned imploring eyes on them, as if begging for help. When she spoke again, her voice shook. "David said this is my last chance. If I don't bring him the files tomorrow…"

She tucked her chin to her chest. When her shoulders started to shake, Micah's heart ached for her.

"This is actually a good thing, Ms. Fox," Brian said reassuringly. "It's always better if the kidnappers want something from you, because then it's not about the child. Hopefully, someone will respond to the Amber Alert any minute, but if not, we know David will get in touch with you. When he does, we'll find out where Owen is. We're going to get your son back, ma'am."

"Thank you." Abigail's eyes were red from crying, but she nodded.

Brian took down her contact information, including the address of her rental home. In Interior, of all places—a street over from where Micah lived. God's hand at work in difficult circumstances, the same way He'd placed him in that store lot at the exact moment his help was needed.

"Let me escort you home," Micah offered as they rose after the interview. "I'm heading to Interior too."

She sniffled. Then took a shuddering breath like it was hard to speak. "Thank you. But don't you have a family to get back to?"

Nope. If there was one thing life had taught him, it was that relationships didn't last. He'd watched the same tragedy play out on repeat, first with his own parents, then for high school and college friends. And when he'd finally met a woman he was willing to risk his own heart for, all he'd gotten was burned.

Taylor had played guitar in the worship band at the little church he attended in Utah when he was stationed out in Arches. She'd caught his eye immediately with her enthusiasm for life, even though she was five years younger. Trouble was, that youthful passion pulled her off to whatever exciting new thing was happening...including the next man.

"No," he told Abigail. "I'm single. It's easier that way with the job."

"Okay." She released a long, defeated sigh. "But I hate imposing on you like this."

"Don't mention it. We'll do everything in our power to get your son back."

An hour later, he pulled to a stop on the street in front of her rental home while she parked in the driveway. She rummaged in her purse for the key and unlocked the front door.

The inside of the place was about what he expected—furnished with a bare-bones living room set and small dining table, old appliances, peeling linoleum on the floor. Not comfortable, but usable. Abigail barely seemed to notice her surroundings as they made trips to the car, carrying in groceries and bags from the trunk. By the time they were done, it'd been over two hours since the

Amber Alert went out, which made it nearly midnight. She kept glancing at her phone, making sure the volume was on.

"Any news from the police?" she asked.

He hated that he had to shake his head.

"You should go home, take care of your groceries. I'll just…put some things away. Try to sleep." She picked up a stuffed lion lying on the couch, squeezing it to her chest.

He held out his hands, not exactly sure what he intended to do, and to his surprise she stepped into his arms and rested her forehead against his shirt. She smelled like raspberries and tears, and her shoulders shook as she wept. Awkwardly, he patted her back. Poor woman had experienced nothing but loss and fear for who knew how many weeks. Maybe longer, given the way she'd described her marriage slowly decaying. She needed a dose of comfort, enough to accept it from a virtual stranger.

"I'm sorry," she said as she pulled back, wiping her cheeks. "I just… I can't stand the thought of him not being here. I feel like I've let him down. Like I f-failed him." A fresh convulsion of sobs racked her body, but she stayed back from him.

"Abigail, it's okay. You've gone through the wringer this evening. You're allowed to cry."

"Thank you." She rubbed her hands on her pants to dry them. "I'll be okay. What about you? Your food is probably rotting in the car by now."

He'd given up on his fresh produce hours ago, but if she wanted some space, he'd give it to her. No matter how much he disliked leaving her alone.

"You've got my number in your contacts," he said as he headed for the door. "And I live a block down on D Street. I can get over here in a flash if you need anything."

As she pulled open the door for him, her phone pinged. Abigail's eyes widened as she pulled it from her pocket.

She stared at the text as he waited impatiently, then held it up for him to read.

Delta Launch Facility, 6 a.m. tomorrow. No cops. Come alone with the files, or... Last chance, Abby.

TWO

Those last words burned into Abigail's retinas until her eyes blurred with tears. *Last chance, Abby.* She didn't need any help figuring out exactly what David meant.

She blinked rapidly as she glanced up at Micah. "I don't have the files. What do I do?"

He already had his phone out. "I'm calling Brian."

"But he said no cops." Her throat tightened. "What if...?" She couldn't bring herself to finish the thought.

"Brian will contact the county sheriff and have units on standby. I'll notify them when we're ready for backup. David won't know. Or, more realistically, he'll expect you to contact the police, but he wants those files badly enough he's going to run the risk." His presence and tone emanated strength and confidence, and she soaked it up like a flower in sunlight. "And he won't know you don't have the files until we get there. Top priority is to make sure Owen's safe. Then we negotiate while we wait for backup."

"Should I go alone?" A tremor rippled up her spine. She'd do it for Owen, no matter how terrifying.

Micah finished tapping out a text on his phone. "No way. You don't know the area, and since he wants those files, he'll hear you out."

"What if something happens to Owen? What if…what if they…?" She fisted her hands, scraping her palms with her nails. The room blurred.

"Trust me, Abigail. We will do everything in our power to protect your son." He stared at his phone for a moment, then looked up at her. "Brian's got everything in hand on his end. I will see you bright and early at 5:30 a.m. tomorrow. Will you be all right?"

His blue eyes searched her face, and she nodded. As much as she hated the thought of the long, sleepless hours ahead, she couldn't ask him to stay. Wouldn't. He'd already been generous enough with his time, and she'd just met the man.

After he left, she closed and locked the front door, sending a cry heavenward even though it might go unheard. *God, please protect Owen.*

Help us get him back safely. She went through the motions of unpacking until exhaustion carried her into an uneasy doze on the hard rental sofa. Before she knew it, knocking at the door snapped her back to reality.

The rising sun had already crested the horizon, chasing away the last hints of pink and purple from the scattered clouds in the west, as she opened the door for Micah. One look at the dark half-moons under his eyes told her he'd slept as fitfully as she had. Today, though, instead of church clothes, he wore a pair of jeans and a T-shirt that left no doubt he spent plenty of time working out. A shoulder holster strapped across his back held a gun, giving her a little extra reassurance. Between his help and the police backup, surely they'd get Owen back.

The thought of hugging her little boy filled her with a sense of longing so sharp it made her eyes burn. How she missed his laundry-soap scent, the rhythmic sound of him sucking his thumb, his big brown eyes staring up at her. The funny things he said. One look at Owen was enough to convince her that every minute of her marriage had been worth it.

The brief tap of Micah's fingers on her arm snapped her back to the moment. "Hey, are you ready?"

She let out a slow breath and nodded, even though her heart raced like a car on the interstate. "What if this doesn't work?"

"Owen is in the Lord's hands, and so are we." He gazed steadily at her. "I don't know if you're a person of faith, but I do know this— He'll never leave us or forsake us. We can trust His promises."

His words soothed the dry, brittle place deep inside her. Was that how she had felt once, long ago? Before her marriage and life circumstances had slowly ground away any hope that God cared?

"I…haven't exactly been on the best terms with God lately. But thank you." She turned away to grab her purse and keys before he could see the tears forming in her eyes. "We should take my car. It has the car seat." She'd buckled Owen into that seat more times than she could count. *Please, God, let me do it again.* The prayer was probably floating up to heaven to sit in the queue with everyone else's, but she couldn't help it. Not with Owen's life on the line.

"Want me to drive?" He stopped in front of her SUV.

She tossed him the keys and climbed into the passenger seat, aware yet again of how much she was relying on this near-total stranger. But he knew the area and the roads, so didn't it make sense to accept his help? Once she had Owen back, she'd figure out her next steps. Somewhere else to run where they could start fresh. She couldn't go to her parents—they'd gladly help, but they were older with health issues, and she couldn't involve them in this mess. Maybe her sister out in Wyoming, though... Eleanor would keep Owen safe, and Abigail could come back for him once she'd convinced these criminals she didn't have what they wanted.

The thought hurt, but Owen's well-being was what mattered most. And right now, he was in jeopardy.

Micah started the engine and backed the car out of the driveway. "The Delta Launch Facility is part of the Minuteman Missile system. It housed nuclear missiles during the Cold War, but now the sites are part of the national park system. North through Badlands and up to the interstate. It'll take us just under half an hour."

Ahead of them, the white, barren ridges of the Badlands jutted out of the prairie like the remnants of a child's sandcastle. To the east, the sun burned like a glowing orange ball against bright blue sky, promising a scorching summer day. Her heart twisted as she thought of Owen—how worried he must be. She squeezed his stuffed lion a little tighter where she clutched it in her lap.

Micah slowed the car as they approached the entrance gate to the national park, but no one was on duty yet. The landscape shifted as they climbed into the park—colorful rock spires and giant buttes loomed close to the car on either side, layers of sediment stacked in strange formations. She'd never seen anything like it. Owen would love it. If…

She gnawed the inside of her cheek. *Don't go there.* She forced her attention to Micah. "How long have you worked here?"

"Two years, heading into my third. I was out at Arches in Utah before this, so I'm used to the desert. Grew up down in Fort Collins. My father still lives there."

"Where does your mom live?" The question popped out before she realized it might not be safe to ask. "Sorry, you don't have to answer that."

He shook his head, flashing her a reassuring smile. "No, it's okay." He cleared his throat. "She left when I was little. For a long time, I thought it was my dad's fault, but kids aren't always the best judges of adult problems. He and I are good now."

"Do you ever hear from her?"

"Nope. She passed soon after she left." He said it casually, but from the way his jaw clenched, the wound must've cut deep. How awful.

But at the look on her face, he shook his head. "Don't go feeling sorry for me. That was a long time ago—" emphasis on the word *long* "—and you've got enough on your plate. Unless I'm helping distract you. Then it's okay."

"Thanks, Micah. I really appreciate what you're doing for me. For us." He was remarkably generous with his time and resources. Sure, he was in law enforcement. Maybe you could say it was his job to help. But the police hadn't offered to escort her home last night. There was nothing in it for him.

"You know," he replied, "there's something about helping other people that makes me feel good. Like I'm living out God's calling in my life. Probably why I wanted to go into the park service. Does that make sense?"

"Yeah, it does. I feel that way too when I'm with my son." His absence pummeled her stomach again, and she crushed the stuffed lion against her chest as if it could keep her from cracking apart. "Before Owen was born, I worked as a preschool teacher. Kids at that age are so fun."

He slowed the car, taking a looping on-ramp onto the interstate. The rugged terrain of the Badlands had been replaced by grass-covered plains. She pointed at a building that flashed past on the right.

"Wait, didn't that say Minuteman...?"

"That was the Visitor Center," Micah said. "We want the Launch Facility a few miles down."

She leaned forward in her seat, straining to see ahead as the miles of empty grassland rolled past. A few minutes later, a small, squat building surrounded by a chain-link fence came into view, some distance from the interstate.

Micah threw on his blinker and slowed the SUV as they approached the exit, then headed north on the narrow county road toward the building. Only one vehicle was in the parking lot—the same black Lincoln Town Car from last night, idling at the far end, its passenger side door ajar.

Her heart lodged in her throat. On the other side of the vehicle, a little blond boy she'd recognize among a thousand stood near a park service placard, poking at something on the sign. Owen. *Thank You, God.* David crouched next to him, the picture of a man who was a trusted family friend, not a traitor.

Micah pulled into a space farther down the lot, and Abigail had her door open when he put his hand on her arm. "Remember what we talked about. Right now, David wants you alive because he thinks you have what he wants. You can't let him think otherwise, or he might decide there's a better way to tie up loose ends. Your goal is to string him along until Owen is safe, and then I'll signal the police. Okay?"

She nodded, her muscles jittery like she'd just gone for a two-mile run. "Got it." Even though her knees quaked, she straightened her spine as her feet hit the pavement. No matter how terrifying this was, she would do it for her son.

"Owen!" His name burst from her lips as she approached the black car. He turned, his eyes going wide.

"Mommy!"

David rose, smiling widely, as if he'd merely been babysitting while she took the night off. He rubbed a hand across Owen's head, ruffling his hair. "Morning, Abigail." He turned to Owen. "See? I told you she'd meet us here."

But when Owen started to take off toward her, David scooped him, swirling him around in a circle like an airplane until he giggled. "Not yet, little man. Mommy has to give me some very important papers first, and then you can go back to her."

Owen's laugh turned to a frown as David set him down, but he stayed put. "Okay, Uncle David."

David's eyes narrowed as he watched her approach. "Where are the files? And I told you to come alone." He nodded toward the SUV, where Micah had climbed out and leaned against the driver's side door with his arms folded across his chest, the straps of his shoulder holster clearly visible.

"He was with me when we got the text," she said, hoping David would accept her non-explanation. "Listen, I know you think I pulled the files when I went to the bank, but I only withdrew cash. The files are still in Chicago."

"Where?"

In a random safe deposit box my husband only told me about after his death, locked with a key I have no idea where to find. She and Eric may have grown increasingly distant over the years, but she'd trusted him. Never thought he was keeping a secret like this, one that could ruin or endanger his family. Now wasn't the right time to think about his betrayal, though. She took a deep breath to calm her racing heart and pulled out the answer she'd rehearsed with Micah.

"In a box at a different bank. I'm the only one who can access it." A lawyer had had to explain the trust to her—how she directly took over all of Eric's property and accounts as the named trustee, without going through probate. That was one thing about being married to an accountant—Eric had been meticulous when it came to finances.

Too bad he hadn't been as careful about his moral choices.

David glanced at the driver of the Town Car, who had climbed out and now faced them, his arms resting on the car's roof, a gun in his hand. It was the same man as yesterday—Vincenzo. He gave a slight shake of his head. Like he didn't believe her.

Abigail dug her fingernails into her palm. "I can get them for you, David. Give me Owen back, and we'll head back to Chicago and take care of it."

David frowned. "Who else knows about the box? Did you tell anyone?"

Her mouth went dry, and she swallowed. What would scare them into keeping her alive but not put anyone else in danger? Not the Chicago cops. For all she knew, they were in cahoots with the mob and that was how they'd learned about the letter and the box. Better to go bigger. "The FBI. They'll get a court order to open it if I don't make it home."

"She's lying," Vincenzo said. "She only told the local cops."

"How do you know?" David asked. Something shifted in his expression, the edges softening until he looked almost...*afraid*. "I can't mess this one up."

Vincenzo laughed and spit on the ground. "You can read it on her face. Or you'd be able to if you weren't letting friendship cloud your judgment. Look at her, she's terrified. You want to solve the problem?" He glanced toward Owen, who scuffed at the dirt with his shoe as he sucked his thumb. The man then made a gun gesture with his empty hand over the car's roof. His message was clear—*shoot her*.

"Wait." Abigail held up her hands. Her whole body trembled. "Let's talk about this. I can get you those files."

David glanced between her and Vincenzo, his brows furrowed. Like he couldn't decide whom to believe. Then his shoulders slumped, and his hand dipped to his waist. "Sorry, Abby, but I can't risk you getting away again."

He pulled out a gun and pointed the barrel directly at her.

* * *

Micah pushed off the SUV and clicked Send on the text he'd had ready to go. Two simple words: Backup now. Brian would have officers here within minutes, probably his and the county sheriff's.

He just needed to keep Abigail and Owen unharmed until then, which meant avoiding any actual shooting. And with both mobsters armed, he and Abigail were at a deadly disadvantage. The goal here was to buy a few minutes' worth of time.

After slipping his phone back into his pocket, he leveled his gun at Vincenzo and advanced across the parking lot, his feet crunching on the pavement. "Hold up. There seems to be some mistake here. You need to let this woman and her kid go."

The driver swiveled his gun onto Micah. "You, stop right there."

"Who *is* that?" David asked.

"He's a…friend." Abigail's voice shook so badly he could hardly hear her. She had to be terrified. And yet she'd had the forethought to keep his personal details secret. Smart woman.

On the far side of David, her son stood with his back pressed against the Minuteman placard. He pulled his thumb out of his mouth and called, "Mommy!"

"You don't need him, David. Please let him go," Abigail urged, her voice thick. "Your business is with me."

David shifted his weight, then glanced between Owen and the driver. "She's right. We don't need the kid. We just need the files. Or her."

Vincenzo nodded. "Fine. Leave the kid here. We can take her back to Chicago and let the *capo* decide what to do with her."

Micah's chest tightened. Letting them drive off with Abigail was *not* how he wanted this to go down, but first priority had to be saving Owen. He walked closer to the vehicle, one slow step at a time, keeping his gun trained on Vincenzo.

"Let the little boy come to me," he said. "I'll get him out of harm's way."

Thank you, Abigail mouthed, relief softening her features.

He grimaced. *Don't thank me yet.* Where were the police? The sirens would hopefully scare the men off, not cause them to panic. But the sooner he could get Owen to safety, the better.

"You put the gun down," Vincenzo ordered,

"then you can keep the kid. The woman is coming with us."

"I'm not lowering this gun until he's safe." Micah resumed his slow steps, giving the front of the car and Vincenzo's weapon a wide berth. Tension made every muscle in his neck and jaw taut. This standoff could go south any second if somebody had a trigger finger.

But nobody flinched as he skirted the front of the car and Vincenzo slowly rotated to track him with the gun. He stopped a dozen feet away from the little boy, who stared at him with wide eyes. The thumb popped out of his mouth. "Who's that guy?" he asked, his little, innocent voice so at odds with the situation.

Micah kept the gun on Vincenzo but glanced at Owen, offering him a warm smile and holding out his hand. "I'm a friend of your mom's. Mr. Micah. She told me all about you."

"Mommy?" The little boy turned to Abigail. "I want to show him my caterpillar." He pointed at the sign, where a two-inch-long fuzzy caterpillar crawled across a black and white photograph of the interior of the launch facility.

"Hurry it up," Vincenzo barked. "We ain't got all day."

"Owen, honey, listen to Mommy," Abigail said. "You need to go with Mr. Micah, okay? I know we don't usually go anywhere with strangers, but he's a good guy." The way her voice cracked tore at Micah's heart. No mother should ever be in this position. *Lord, please get all three of us out of here alive.*

Owen frowned, his lip quivering again. David shifted his weight like he was growing agitated.

"Do what Mommy says, Owen," Abigail commanded, her voice stronger this time. Finally, the child took a shuffling step toward Micah—first one foot, then the other, until he stood directly in front of him with his head turned down toward his feet.

Micah placed a hand on the little blond head and ruffled his hair. "Come with me, buddy." Then to the men, he said, "I'm going to back away with him now toward that SUV, and once he's safe, I'll lower my gun." He took Owen's hand and led him away, walking backward to keep his weapon aimed at Vincenzo.

They were halfway to the SUV when the faint sound of sirens reached Micah's ears. *Thank You, Lord.* But how was this going to play out? He picked up his pace, pushing Owen toward the vehicle.

"Wait, what's that?" Vincenzo cocked his head in the direction of the interstate.

"You told the cops, didn't you?" David asked.

Tension wrapped around Micah's ribs as he picked up Owen and dashed around the SUV.

"No," Abigail's voice carried across the parking lot, "I didn't. Someone must've recognized your vehicle. You're wanted for kidnapping."

Vincenzo swore loudly. "Get her in the car. Now."

His instinct was to deposit Owen on the ground and run back to stop them, but he couldn't leave the child out here. *Get the boy to safety,* then *help Abigail.* He opened the front passenger door, set Owen on the floor, and crouched to meet his wide brown gaze. "Did you know prairie dogs live in little burrows under the ground? I want you to pretend you're a prairie dog and this is your home. Can you do that?"

Owen sat down, tucking his knees into his chest. "Like this?"

"Yeah." He handed the little boy the stuffed lion Abigail had left on the seat. "I'll be right back."

By now the sirens were clearly audible. He peered around the back of the SUV, gun in hand. Vincenzo had already slid into the driver's seat. David had the rear door open, and Abigail's dark ginger hair flashed into view as he shoved her into the car. A band tightened around Micah's chest.

No. He couldn't let them drive off with her, or Owen would lose his mother. She'd vanish into the Chicago underworld. *If* they survived the car chase and didn't decide to kill her before they even made it out of South Dakota.

"Freeze!" He stepped out from behind the SUV and aimed the gun at David where he stood with one foot inside the open door. Taking a shot from here would be an unacceptable risk, with Abigail right behind his target. Hopefully the other man wouldn't recognize that fact.

But David shook his head. "You got the kid. We're taking Abigail."

The front passenger side window rolled down and Vincenzo's gun flashed. Micah dove for cover behind the SUV as the other man fired, shattering a rear window. From inside the vehicle, Owen squealed.

"Owen, stay down!" Micah called to him, praying the child would listen. Across the parking lot, the car door slammed shut. Sirens blared. Far across the prairie, red-and-blue lights flashed as police cars streamed down the exit ramp from the freeway, but they weren't close enough. Not when these men might get desperate, decide to shoot Abigail, and dump her body.

The black sedan's engine roared to life. Its tires squealed as Vincenzo hit the gas. Micah crouched behind the SUV, taking a couple of last desperate shots at the tires as the car flew past.

But as the shots fell short and the car peeled out of the parking lot, all he could think was one thing. Owen would grow up without a mother, and it was *his* fault.

He'd failed.

THREE

Gravel crunched beneath the tires and shots echoed outside as the car lurched forward, throwing Abigail backward in the seat. She drew a ragged gasp and strained to look over her shoulder. Was Micah still alive?

And Owen…was he hurt? All she wanted was to hug her little boy close and vanish somewhere far away from these men who wouldn't leave her alone. Was it so much to ask after all she'd been through? Why couldn't God, who'd created the entire world and orchestrated all of human history, manage to protect her and her son?

Because He doesn't care, she thought bitterly. Not about her and Owen.

But that meant she had to look out for Owen herself, and unless she wanted him to grow up an orphan, she had to get out of this car. Now. She slid closer to the edge of the seat, her hand creeping toward the door handle.

"Punch it," David ordered from the back seat, gesturing wildly in the direction of the interstate. "We can't go that way, too many cops."

Vincenzo swore. "Don't you think I see 'em? Hold on." He cranked the steering wheel to the left, hitting the brakes as the car swerved on loose gravel and nearly veered off the road. He overcorrected, bringing the car too far left, and Abigail seized her chance.

Yanking the door open, she launched out of the vehicle as David yelled behind her. The ground flew up to meet her and she landed hard on her right shoulder, her face digging into bristly grass and sand as she rolled like a tumbleweed.

Her body came to a halt, leaving her face-down on the ground. Everything hurt. From nearby, the sound of the car engine shifted as Vincenzo braked. The electric whirr of the window sent a jolt of adrenaline through her system. The black barrel of Vincenzo's gun appeared.

"Abigail!" Micah yelled, his voice muted by the approaching sirens.

She launched forward at the same moment a sharp crack sounded. Dirt flew up, pelting her in the back as she scrambled away from the car. Police cruisers barreled down the road, and David's panicked voice carried from the black sedan. "Go! Go!"

The black car's tires spun as it launched forward again, heading away from the interstate, pursued by two of the cruisers. Two others screeched to a halt on the road a half dozen yards away.

Feet pounded across the ground and a moment later Micah was by her side, crouching next to her, his hand warm and solid on her back. "Are you all right?"

She drew in a shuddering breath but managed to nod. He helped her shift her weight until she was sitting. They watched as one of the police cars turned around and headed for the freeway, while an officer got out of the other.

Now that the immediate danger was over, her entire body felt limp like a spaghetti noodle. But she couldn't relax yet. "Owen! Where's Owen? Is he safe?"

"I'll go get him. You'd better stay here until EMS arrives to make sure you're okay. That was a hard crash."

Was it? Now that he mentioned it, the ebb of adrenaline had left her upper body aching in its wake, especially the side that had taken the impact. She felt gingerly along her shoulder as the officer approached and introduced himself.

"Try not to move, ma'am," he said as he knelt next to her. He ripped open the package for an emergency blanket, took out the thin, shiny sheet, and draped it over her back. "We'll need to get you and your son to the hospital to make sure you're all right."

Owen. Thinking about him sent another surge of cortisol spiking through her system, and she almost launched back to her feet, but there was Micah, strong and capable as he carried her little boy across the grass. Owen had his arms wrapped around Micah's neck. When he saw her, he pushed away and held out both arms.

Micah held him firmly until they'd reached her side. "Mommy got hurt," he explained, "so we have to be gentle."

"Does she need a kiss?" Owen asked, his mouth pulling down at the corners.

"If you're really careful." Micah set him down, and the little boy tottered up to Abigail. She held out her good arm, and when he stepped against her, she pulled him close until her senses filled with the soft scent and warmth of him.

Thank you, God. At least He'd given her

back her little boy. A tiny shoot of green in the dry winter of her soul.

Her gaze met Micah's over the top of Owen's head, and a smile tugged at his lips, making a dimple appear in his cheek above the beard. How was a man as kind, capable, and handsome as him still single? And how had he gotten so good with kids?

Not that his dating status mattered to her. *At all.* Even if the cops caught David, she and Owen would have to keep moving around until the mob either gave up or their entire operation was shut down.

Besides, if there was one thing she'd learned from her years with Eric, it was that she'd never willingly put herself through that kind of misery again. She'd had such high hopes when they started dating, and when he proposed only six months later, his offer seemed like everything she'd been looking for. God's provision for a lifetime of security and love.

But within days of tying the knot, she realized she'd been looking at him through rose-colored glasses, seeing what she wanted to see instead of reality. Time only confirmed that they weren't remotely suited for each other. She'd held on to every Biblical marriage principle, determined to honor God and her husband and make the marriage work, and what had she gotten for it? A husband who, although he'd never cheated on her or abused her, had slowly withdrawn from the relationship to invest himself in work, leaving her heartbroken and alone in the empty shell of their vows. Worse, he'd gotten tangled up with the mafia—and now they were coming after her and Owen.

No, there was no way she could entrust her heart to another man, regardless of the butterflies skipping through her insides at his smile.

But certainly, Micah wasn't thinking anything along these lines about *her*, so she smiled warmly as she held Owen close. "Thank you for everything you did. For saving him for me."

"Of course," he replied. "I couldn't have done anything else."

When the ambulance arrived, the EMTs helped Abigail and Owen into the back. Micah followed in her SUV as they drove to a hospital in Rapid City. The ER doctor examined her shoulder, determining she'd only strained it during the fall, and administered IVs to both her and Owen for dehydration. The little boy balked at the needle until the doctor explained it was like a straw for his arm. "So your body gets a drink."

They were resting comfortably in one of

the small rooms off the ER, Owen curled up beside her in the stiff hospital bed, when Micah returned with Detective Overton.

"Glad to see you back with your son." The detective smiled warmly as he took a seat next to the hospital bed. "This won't take too long—I just need to get your testimony, and Owen's too, if he's willing to talk about what happened. Otherwise, we can wait until tomorrow."

"Let's try now," she said, tracing a finger gently across Owen's cheek. Better to get this over with and get him home. He'd been through enough already, and once he was asleep and she was alone, she'd be able to come up with some sort of plan to get them away from here. Maybe Detective Overton could help her escape the mob, but after her experience with the Chicago police, she knew better than to leave her and Owen's safety entirely up to the authorities. No, she needed to think for herself.

Their lives depended on it.

Hearing Owen's testimony was almost harder than listening to Abigail's. Micah leaned against the wall of the small room, his fingers scratching absently at the short bristly hair of his beard. The little boy was groggy when she first woke him up, but soon he launched into a retelling of what had happened, complete with all the things a child notices—how he woke up in the morning in "Uncle David's" car but there wasn't a car seat, the hash browns and ketchup he had for breakfast, and ending with the caterpillar he'd found on a sign in the parking lot and *Mommy, could we keep it as a pet*?

Kids had an amazing level of resilience. But so did Abigail, it seemed. She'd weathered some horrible things in the preceding months, and she wasn't done yet. Every minute with her made him more determined to help her and make sure she and Owen were safe.

But realistically, protecting and helping her was Brian's job, not his. In fact, as Brian explained to her, anything outside of Rapid City wasn't even *his* jurisdiction—instead, he'd be coordinating with Sheriff Dan Layton on the case.

And Micah? He was a park ranger. Maybe in law enforcement, yes, but not a cop, and this situation definitely didn't count as national park business. Still, there was only so much anyone could officially do, and if she'd let him, he wanted to help pick up the slack.

A few hours later, Abigail and Owen were discharged from the hospital. At Brian's recommendation, they stopped by a local store and picked up a burner phone for Abigail in case the mob was tracking her other device. Then Micah drove them back to Interior. By the time they reached her rental an hour away, both she and Owen were out cold despite it being midday. The fact she felt safe enough to fall asleep warmed his chest. He sat for a moment, letting the car idle in the driveway and listening to the soft sound of Owen sucking his thumb.

Was this what it would've been like to have a family of his own? Even watching Abigail's relationship with Owen made a place inside his chest ache. Had *his* mother ever felt that way about him? Like she'd move heaven and earth to get back to him?

He sincerely doubted it, not with the way she'd abandoned him when he was eight. Just packed up and left without a word, like he was an extra clothes hanger she didn't need to take. Not worth her time or effort. Had she ever regretted that choice? Or had death claimed her before she had the chance?

And what about Owen, who would grow up without a father?

He cut the engine and gently shook Abigail's shoulder. "Hey, we're back. Let's get you and Owen inside."

As he escorted her to the door, his phone pinged with a text notification from Brian.

Suspects abandoned the vehicle in Wall and escaped on foot. Search is ongoing. Layton is sending a patrol car to watch Abigail's home, ETA 15.

He glanced up at Abigail, his stomach slipping toward his knees. "I'm sorry, Abigail. David got away."

Her knuckles whitened against Owen's back, and she kissed the top of his head where it rested against her shoulder. "What do I do now?" She glanced both ways up the street, as if she expected David or Vincenzo to materialize again any second.

He gritted his teeth. No one should have to live in this kind of fear. "Sheriff Layton has a patrol car coming to keep watch. The officer should be here in fifteen minutes. I'll stay until they arrive, but then I've got to check in at work." He'd called in earlier when it'd become obvious that he wouldn't make his 9:00 a.m. shift at Ben Reifel Visitor Center. Yet unless he wanted to use up a vacation day, they'd expect him to appear eventually. Especially considering Abigail was not family and her situation was not under his jurisdiction.

Once the patrol car arrived, he exchanged a quick word with the officer and told Abigail goodbye, promising to check on her later. Leaving her and Owen alone was harder than it should've been, but she'd assured him she'd be fine. Forty-five minutes later, he'd changed into his uniform and made it to his desk, but he couldn't shake a lingering sense of unease at leaving her.

Not my business. What *was* his business was this growing stack of paperwork he needed to process, along with assisting in planning the prairie burn scheduled for next week and investigating a mule deer poaching report that had come in that morning. Normally he loved his job, but now the hours dragged by slower than a paleontology dig.

The next two days were more of the same—going about his day-to-day work, periodically checking in with Abigail, finding that she was doing fine without him.

Maybe it was time to accept that Sheriff Layton and Brian had things well in hand, and he could stop worrying.

He couldn't let himself get attached…like he had with Taylor. He hadn't learned she was dating another man at the same time until *after* he'd proposed.

The pain and humiliation of that moment,

the pity on her face as she'd said, *"I'm so sorry, Micah, I thought you knew I wasn't serious about you..."* Over two years later, the memory still scorched his insides.

He would *never* put himself in that position again.

That resolution flew out the window the second his cell phone rang, displaying Abigail's new number. "Micah here," he answered. "What's up?"

"The police car is gone." Her voice shook so badly he could barely understand her, and she paused, exhaling slowly. When she spoke again, she'd cobbled together some measure of calm. "I don't know how long, but there was one before lunch. I just noticed now when Owen wanted to go outside to play."

Heat sparked in his stomach. Why had they pulled the car without notifying him or Abigail? And what could possibly justify the decision?

"I'm going to make some calls, and we'll figure out what's going on," he said, keeping his tone calm. "Why don't you and Owen stay inside for now, and be sure to lock the door and keep away from the windows, okay? This should only take a few minutes."

Silence for a moment, then she released another breath. "Okay."

After hanging up, he punched in the number for the county sheriff. The office assistant patched him through to the sheriff's phone.

"Dan Layton," the sheriff answered. Micah offered up a silent prayer of thanks that the man was in his office.

"Sheriff, this is Ranger Micah Ellis over in Badlands. I've been assisting Brian Overton from RCPD with the Abigail Fox kidnapping case."

"Sure, what can I do for you?" Layton asked, his voice as leathery and tough as a piece of bison jerky. Micah had met him once, a few months after he'd started at Badlands, but they'd never had any cause to work together. "If you're looking for an update, you can be sure we'll notify RCPD as soon as we have one."

"No, actually, I'm calling because the patrol officer who's supposed to be outside Abigail Fox's home in Interior isn't there."

"That's right."

Micah frowned, waiting for the sheriff to follow up with an explanation, but he remained silent. After a moment, he prodded, "Why isn't an officer there, like we agreed?"

"You mean, like Detective Overton and I agreed?"

A jab to remind him of his place. Even

though his insides bristled, Micah kept his tone calm. "Of course."

"We've concluded she and her son are no longer in danger."

What? The irritation in his stomach flared into anger. "But how? Her kid was—"

"Look, Ranger Evans—"

"Ellis," Micah said firmly.

"I don't have time to discuss this case with you, nor frankly do you have any jurisdiction over it to begin with. If you want to know more, reach out to RCPD. Good day."

The line went dead. Micah gripped the phone a little tighter than necessary as he jabbed Brian Overton's number into the keypad.

Relief washed through him when Brian picked up. It didn't take long to relate his conversation with the sheriff. "Is he always that surly and unhelpful?" he finished.

"He *has* been in law enforcement for over thirty years." Brian chuckled, but it sounded forced. "Sorry about all of this. I spoke with him an hour ago but got tied up in a meeting before I could call you. Layton got in touch with Abigail's contact at Chicago PD, Officer Jimmy Bernetto. He says they've got feelers out on the Eric Fox case and word is, the mob is dropping it after the failed kidnapping effort. Apparently, David Blakely and his side-kick have been ordered home."

"Do *you* trust that report?" Micah narrowed his eyes. Was Abigail's safety worth the risk if their informant was wrong?

"He's a fellow officer, Micah. Of course, we're going to trust him. Besides, we haven't dropped the case. Bernetto and his men are on the lookout for Blakely, and if they pick him up, we'll press charges. Otherwise...the mob has their own twisted form of justice. Blakely's not going to be harassing Abigail again."

"Okay, but shouldn't we keep the patrol car out there until those men are confirmed back in Chicago?"

Brian sighed. "It's up to Layton. Remember, this isn't my jurisdiction. Or yours," he said pointedly. "Unless it happens on park property, it falls under the county. Okay?"

Micah clenched his jaw. "Obviously." What did Brian think he was going to do? Sit outside her house in an NPS vehicle? That would never fly with the chief ranger.

After hanging up, he dropped his face into his hands and massaged his forehead. Truth was, he'd been worried about Abigail and Owen for two days now. He hadn't wanted to invade their space, but this afternoon, hearing how hard she was struggling to control her voice… She was scared, and he wasn't convinced this news would do much to alleviate her fears. Not after everything she'd been through.

He sighed and picked up his cell. Better to get this over with. But before he could open his contacts, the phone rang. His throat tightened when he glanced at the screen. It was Abigail's number again.

She didn't even wait for him to speak. "Did they send a plainclothes officer?" Her voice trembled. Then, away from the phone, "Owen, stay back from the window." The little boy whined in the background.

"No, they pulled the patrol. Abigail, what's going on?"

"A car just parked out front. Different than David's. White, four doors. Two men in the front who I haven't seen before. Watching the house."

She paused, her breath rattling through the phone, fear emanating out of her like smoke from a fire. "Micah, they're getting out of the car."

Abigail's heart thrashed against her ribs like it was trying to escape. "What do I do?" she managed to choke out. Was there any chance she was overreacting? That they were merely neighbors? That wasn't a risk she could take, not with Owen.

"The back door." Micah's low, strong voice brought a sense of calm to her racing heart. "Take Owen and go out the back now. Head north between the houses to the next street. D Street. Third house on the left. It has a striped awning over the front entry. Key's in the fake rock behind the flowerpot."

"North, D Street, awning," she repeated, hoping those directions would make sense once they were running.

"I'm leaving now. Should be to you in fifteen." He paused. "Abigail, you can do this."

She exhaled slowly, even though her ribs felt like someone had cinched a tourniquet around them. "See you soon."

After ending the call, she stuffed the phone into her back pocket, grabbed her purse, and scooped Owen up. "Come on, bud, we're going for a walk."

"But I don't have my water bottle!" he protested as she dashed with him through the small kitchen to the slider at the back of the house.

"We'll get a drink at Mr. Micah's house."

Midday sun blasted down on her head as she slipped through the door and took off across the backyard. Between the pounding of her feet on the hard ground came distant thumps—the men knocking at her door? It wouldn't take long before they realized she and Owen were gone.

She dashed across the backyards of neighboring houses as she headed north, keeping behind storage sheds and fences as much as possible, and avoiding the exposed, open desert in the center of the block. Finally she burst onto the next street parallel to hers.

There, just like he'd said—the third house on the left had an awning. Her arms burned, and she forced her feet to a walk as she carried Owen across the street. Just in case anyone was watching. No sign of the men yet, but they'd be utterly conspicuous out here.

She didn't put Owen down until they reached Micah's porch. "Stay right here," she told him as she fished the key out of the fake rock.

Tension knotted around her midsection as she jammed the key into the lock, praying the door would open. Then the latch clicked, and she could breathe again. She pushed the door open, retreated inside with Owen, and locked up behind them.

And not a moment too soon, because farther down the street, the same white car turned onto Micah's road and slowly drove past the houses like a circling vulture. Each breath felt too loud, despite the fact there was no possible way the driver could hear them. She clutched Owen close, standing on tiptoe to watch through the glass at the top of the door. When the car passed the house, she turned and slumped against the door, pressing her face against Owen's head.

He pushed against her, struggling to get down. "Mommy, where are we?"

Her arms, which felt like lead weights, released him almost on their own, and her injured shoulder ached. "We're at Mr. Micah's house. The good guy who helped me find you the other day."

The house was similar to hers—a small ranch with an attached carport to one side—and like hers, they'd entered directly into the living room. A far cry from her beautiful home in Chicago, but for a single man, Micah had decorated the small space tastefully. Neutral leather furniture sat grouped around a striking wood coffee table that looked like it had been hewn from a large tree. The walls were decorated with vintage National Park posters and a pair of floating shelves lined with wooden model airplanes.

Owen kicked his shoes off and drifted

away from her, taking small, cautious steps. Like he was afraid of getting in trouble—or worse, nabbed again—any second. Her heart ached for him. *Lord, if You care about my son, please help him forget this ordeal.* Kids were resilient—he'd get through this—but everything that had happened would leave a mark. How could it not?

"It's okay, bud," she said, her voice catching. "We're safe here."

But as the white car circled past again, she couldn't help hoping that Micah would hurry.

Micah made it to Abigail's street in a record six minutes, but only because he'd pushed the speed limit by a few miles per hour. There was no sign of the white car—had they checked her home and given up already? She'd texted him as soon as she made it to his house, so at least he knew she was safe.

The front door to her house was ajar. He pulled up on the street and shut off the engine, then drew his gun from its holster in case someone was still inside. The exterior looked quiet, and no movement was apparent as he cautiously approached the front door. He paused on the doorstep, surveying the disaster that was before him. Abigail's entire living room had been tossed—not that she had much—but now the contents of all her bags and boxes lay strewn throughout the room.

So the mob had given up, had they? He ground his teeth as he picked his way across the room. He'd made it to the kitchen, where the open slider showed Abigail's escape route, when thumps behind him made him turn.

A dark-haired man darted from the back hallway and sprinted for the front door.

"Stop!" Micah yelled, chasing after him, but the man ignored him and bolted out the front door.

Seconds later a white car pulled up and the man rolled over the hood to escape into the passenger side door. Tires squealed as the vehicle vanished around the bend. Micah fisted his hand into a ball, holstered his gun, and pulled out his cell. After updating the sheriff's department and Brian, he drove to his house.

"They must not have believed you about the files," he told Abigail once he'd locked his doors, sat her down, and explained what happened.

"I don't have them." She pressed her hands to her cheeks. "I don't know what it will take to convince them. But I do know this. Owen isn't safe here. Not if the police don't believe me."

"Sheriff Layton has an officer on the way,"

Micah replied. "But if you had family who could take Owen..." He frowned, watching the boy as he flipped through the big coffee table book of airplanes Micah had held on to since his own childhood. Abigail wasn't safe yet, either. And while she might buy a little safety going on the run again with Owen, at least here people could help.

People like *him*.

She stood, pacing the room. "I'll have to think about it. In the meantime, is it safe to go back to my house? See what they took?"

"They drove off, but we need to be careful not to disturb anything before the police arrive."

Once they reached her rental, Abigail stared in silence at the disaster in her living room. Owen pushed against her, trying to get down, but she held him close.

"Mommy, why is it so messy?" he asked. "And where's my lion?"

"We'll find him, honey, but we can't touch anything yet. The police have to come first."

He stuck his thumb in his mouth and rested his head on her shoulder, then mumbled words Micah almost didn't catch. "I miss Daddy."

"Oh, sweet pea, me too," she murmured.

His heart hurt. Poor kid. And Abigail too—

losing a spouse was a life-changing event. He'd witnessed the wreckage firsthand in his father's life. And the pain Owen must feel? He didn't even get to hope his dad might come back, not the way eight-year-old Micah had clung to that possibility when *his* mother left.

Fifteen minutes later, three officers arrived from the sheriff's department. Together they combed through the house, searching for evidence and missing items.

"Just my laptop bag," Abigail said wearily. "It had my computer and some loose papers. Bills, personal correspondence. The laptop is password protected, but I doubt it will take long for them to find a way to hack it. There's a picture of Eric's letter on my hard drive."

"But the letter doesn't give the safe deposit box's location, does it?" Micah asked. He glanced at the three officers working on the other side of the room.

"No. Maybe Eric was worried the letter would be intercepted, and he intended to tell me himself but never got to it. Or maybe he left some clue back at my house in Chicago and I just missed it."

"Or could there be a clue in the letter itself?"

"Let me grab it. It's here in my purse." She

riffled around in her bag for a moment, then pulled out a folded piece of paper.

He took it and gingerly opened it.

Dearest Abs,
If you're receiving this letter, it means I saw the end coming and ran out of time to explain. Sometimes there aren't enough words anyway.
 I'm so sorry for how I've failed you and Owen. If I could go back, there are so many decisions I'd make differently. I know that doesn't mean much now, but you have the chance to make things right. I've named you as trustee for everything, including the safe deposit box. Should make the transition easiest. You'll know what to do.
 Remember that night in Key West? Conch sandwiches and karaoke. Wish life didn't have to move so fast. So many missed opportunities.
Yours,
Eric.

The edges of the paper were well-worn and tattered, like she'd held this page tightly and read it over and over, a visible reminder of everything she'd lost. His heart ached for her as he handed the note back.

"See?" she asked. "He mentions the box but doesn't say where it is. I thought maybe he meant Key West, but I called around to banks there and no one had heard of him. I've wracked my brain to come up with what else he could've meant, but I can't think of anything."

"This is what you showed the Chicago cops?"

"Right. Officer James Bernetto. He handled the Chicago break-in too. But I can't figure out how David knew about the letter. Unless Eric told him?" Her eyes lost focus for a moment, as if she was drifting back into old memories.

"Maybe," he agreed, but something about the whole scenario didn't sit right. If the sheriff had contacted this same Officer Bernetto, and he was the one who told them the mob had given up *right* before men showed up at her house…was it too big of a leap to wonder if the mob had bought him off? But there was no reason to scare Abigail. Better to let the idea simmer, maybe discuss it later with Brian.

He stood with her on the porch as the police left after wrapping up the crime scene investigation. She pressed her hands to her cheeks as two of the cruisers drove away, leaving the third parked across the street, assigned by the sheriff to renew the patrol. "What am I going to do now?"

The question was muttered so low it was probably meant to be rhetorical, but fire sparked in Micah's chest. No way was he going to wait for Brian and Sheriff Layton to find the evidence they needed to take action. Or worse, leave her to solve this mess for herself. She'd been struggling on her own long enough.

He turned to her, his jaw set. "I'm going to help you, Abigail. We'll find a way to get Owen to safety, and then we're going to figure out where your husband stashed those files and get them into the hands of the FBI. Together."

Something flickered in her wide green eyes as she studied him, like she was debating the offer. Out of politeness? Consideration for what it might cost him? But now wasn't the time to be polite, not when her safety was on the line.

She shook her head. "I couldn't—"

"Yes, you could," he insisted. "Besides, I have too many vacation days anyway. I need to use some of them up. You'd be helping me out."

He could see the exact moment she yielded. Her shoulders went from ramrod straight to relaxed, and a tiny smile curled at her lips. The closest thing to hope he'd seen yet on her face. "Okay. I… I'm kind of lost right now. I… Thank you, Micah."

The soft way she said his name, the fragile hope etched in her eyes, tugged at some protective place deep inside. The urge to pull her into an embrace swept over him, but he stuffed his hands in his pockets. Hadn't he learned his lesson with Taylor? He'd felt the same way about her when they first met. She'd been lugging an electric guitar, a stack of music books, *and* an amp into church for worship band—hauling way too much at once—and he'd hustled up the sidewalk to lend a hand. The look of gratitude she'd given him would've melted any man. Unfortunately, he'd been too blind to see he wasn't the only one on the receiving end of those looks.

No, helping Abigail wasn't about feelings or relationships or him and her. It was about stepping up to help this person God had placed in his path.

That was it.

And he'd keep reminding himself of that fact every single day until Abigail was safe and they could go their separate ways.

FOUR

Abigail woke to bright sunlight piercing the blinds over her head. Owen slept next her, snuggled under the covers with his stuffed lion, his mouth hanging open and eyes sealed shut. She smiled, her insides filling with warmth, until she remembered what the day held in store. A heavy sense of dread chased away the lazy contentment, and suddenly it was all she could do to prevent herself from hugging Owen tight and never letting go.

But that wouldn't do. He needed his sleep. She glanced at the clock—7:00 a.m.—then slipped out from under the covers and tiptoed into the bathroom to get ready. In a few short hours Micah would arrive to escort her and Owen to the location they'd chosen to meet her sister. The decision had gutted Abigail, but it wasn't safe for Owen to stay here. *With her.* She'd had to explain all of it to Eleanor—

her suspicions about Eric's death, the police investigation, the mobsters after her.

Somehow she'd become one of those women on TV talk shows who attracted constant danger and couldn't reliably care for her child. Her insides twisted, and she forced her trembling fingers through the motions of combing her hair and applying enough makeup to look like she was at least trying to keep herself together.

By the time she was done, the soft padding of feet in the hallway told her Owen was awake.

"Hey, sleepyhead." She tugged him into a tight embrace.

He giggled, his smile huge beneath puffy eyes, as he melted into her side. How was she going to let him go? Until all this started, they'd never been apart for more than a few hours at a time. Why was God letting this happen to her?

Micah arrived long before she had any answers. Owen ran up to him as she let him inside their small house.

"Mr. Micah, look at my backpack!" He turned around, displaying his small red backpack with the lobster claws and two googly eyes on the ends of fabric antennae.

Micah dropped down onto a knee. "Whoa,

it's a lobster! That's awesome, Owen. Do you have one for me?"

"No, Mr. Micah, you're silly!" Owen laughed, and light sparked in Micah's blue eyes. He glanced up at Abigail, his expression softening, and when he stood, he reached toward her, his fingers falling just shy of touching her arm.

"You okay?" he asked.

The gentle question tightened the knot that had been building inside her chest all morning, and she clenched her teeth together as she nodded. Anything to keep from crying in front of him again. Or upsetting Owen.

It took a moment for the burning in her eyes to subside, but then she pasted on a fake smile that hopefully hid the storm inside. "Owen's got everything packed for his big trip to stay with Aunt Eleanor."

"That's right." Owen's small chest puffed out. "Mommy says I'm so big I get to go without her."

"You sure do," Micah replied. "Let's take your things out to the car."

Abigail handed him Owen's small duffel, stuffed with the meager selection of clothes, books, and toys she'd managed to cobble together before leaving Chicago. Eleanor was still single and wouldn't have much on hand to keep a little boy occupied, but she *did* work for a therapeutic horse ranch out in Wyoming, and she knew kids. Owen would be fine.

Her hands shook anyway as she buckled Owen into his seat. Micah stowed Owen's bag in the back seat then ducked across the street to tell the patrol officer they'd be back in a few hours. He'd already notified Detective Overton and Sheriff Layton, so extra security could be on standby, just in case.

She tossed the keys to Micah and climbed into the passenger seat. How many times had she sat here, with Owen in the back, as Eric had driven them somewhere? A bittersweet feeling of nostalgia warmed her chest for a fleeting second before reality crashed back in. Eric had put her in this awful position, and the man driving her now—out of the goodness of his heart—certainly wasn't going to be a fixture in her and Owen's lives. Micah was probably counting down the minutes until he could escape from the dangerous mess her life had become.

But as they headed north through the park toward the interstate, she couldn't help but marvel at his way with Owen. Or how comfortable her son seemed to feel with him.

"Mr. Micah," he asked, "why isn't there any grass on those mountains?" He traced a finger across the window, leaving a smear on the glass.

"That's a great question, Owen. It's because of a few reasons, but mostly because the sides are so steep the water runs right down. If any plants tried to grow, they wouldn't have anything to drink. But it means we get to see all the colors of the rock layers. Pretty cool, huh?"

"Mmm-hmm." And a few minutes later, as they climbed higher into the park, "Why are the rocks shaped so weird?"

"Kind of like big sculptures, aren't they?" Micah smiled, making the dimple pop in his cheek. *Not* a helpful observation.

Abigail turned her attention back to the landscape.

"Even though you usually think of rock as very hard, these rocks are actually quite soft," he explained. "Wind and rain have changed their shape over time. But I like to think of them as God's artwork."

"I like that too. So does Mommy. Right, Mommy?"

"I like whatever you like." She turned in the seat and tickled Owen's leg, wishing there was some way to imprint his happy laughter on her memory forever.

This arrangement was only temporary,

though. Just until she and Micah figured out what the mob wanted and got those files to the authorities. A week, maybe two at the most. She wouldn't let her thoughts go to all the ways things could go wrong, or the possibility of a drawn-out trial and witness protection and Owen being away from her longer.

They reached the small town of Wall far too soon, and Micah steered the SUV off the interstate and into the crowded parking lot outside Wall Drug. Huge signs plastered the exterior of the big building advertising T-shirts, ice cream, a museum, and an eighty-foot dinosaur. She and Micah and Eleanor had gone back and forth over the best location to make the exchange. Eleanor had volunteered to drive all the way to Interior, until Micah had pointed out how much easier it would be to track her vehicle if anyone was secretly keeping watch on Abigail's house.

At least at a tourist trap like Wall Drug, where hundreds of cars came and went all day long, they had a shot at slipping in and out unnoticed.

As Micah pulled into a spot, Abigail pointed at a giant sculpture of a rabbit with antlers standing in an open courtyard between sections of the store. "Is that a…?"

"Jackalope?" He laughed. "Yep. Now you've

seen the real attraction of South Dakota. It isn't the Badlands or Mount Rushmore."

The twinkle in his eye made her smile as she got out of the car and pulled Owen from his car seat. For a second, an image flitted through her mind of the three of them coming here just for fun, of taking Owen's picture with the jackalope, of eating ice cream and buying T-shirts and doing something normal.

Then she shook her head, unnerved at how easily Micah had fit into that vision. A relationship with him—or any man, for that matter—was so far out of the question it wasn't even worth considering. Especially a man she'd just met. Hadn't she learned anything from rushing into marriage with Eric? She'd have to be extra guarded with her thoughts.

Micah closed the driver's side door and nodded toward Owen. "What about the car seat? Does your sister need it?"

"No, she's borrowing a booster seat from a friend. I figured it would be easier." She grabbed Owen's small duffel from the floor and tucked his arms through his backpack straps.

Micah locked the car, handed her the keys, and checked his wristwatch. "We're twenty minutes early. I-c-e c-r-e-a-m?" he spelled out.

"What does that mean?" Owen asked. Micah winked at her, unleashing an unwelcome flurry of butterflies in her stomach. It was rather unfortunate he had to be so attractive.

"Sure," she said. "Let's do it."

"It spells ice cream," he told Owen. "Want some?"

"Yes!" the little boy squealed. "I like strawberry best. Mommy loves chocolate."

"I sure do." She held her palm out to him. "Hold my hand, okay?"

"And Mr. Micah's!" He offered Micah a huge smile and slipped his hand into Micah's larger one. The simple, trusting action tore at Abigail's heart. How her little boy must miss his father—though Eric had been absent so much these past several months. Whatever the case, Owen was soaking up Micah's attention like a desert plant in the rain.

"Here, let me carry the bag." Micah held out his other hand, and she passed the duffel to him. He led the way into the courtyard, past the jackalope and a roaring animatronic T-rex, and through a door into what looked like a nineteenth-century Western street, complete with storefront facades and streetlights.

She glanced at Micah. "You weren't making that up about this place being huge."

"Nope." He grinned.

The place was a maze of specialty shops

and souvenirs, and she squeezed Owen's hand a little tighter as they navigated past racks of T-shirts, shelves of leather moccasins, and glass cases full of pocketknives. Tourists filled the gaps between displays and spilled out of doorways in noisy groups.

"It's busy in here. I'd better carry you, bud," she said to Owen, scooping him up.

"The place is usually packed," Micah said, his voice low and close to her ear. "But there should be extra officers in here." He scanned the room as they rounded a bend. "Must be plainclothes, because I only see the usual Wall Drug security."

She followed his gaze and noticed a man in a black uniform standing against a wall, a red-and-white badge on his shirtsleeve displayed the word "Security" in large print. She breathed a little easier. As Micah guided them past shot glasses, T-shirts, and old apothecary bottles, she kept Owen's little hands out of reach of breakable objects. Finally, they stepped into a smaller space set up like an old-fashioned soda fountain. There was a long counter with stools, and several small tables dotted the room beneath stained-glass Tiffany lamps.

Micah went to place the order while Abigail sat with Owen at one of the tables. Her fingers itched to check her phone to see if Eleanor had arrived yet, but she'd given her sister Micah's number and left the prepaid phone at home out of an abundance of caution.

Owen chatted away about the funny decorations on the walls, but Abigail only half-listened. Now that they were here, the moment when she'd have to part with him felt too imminent. She wanted to squeeze him close and never let go, but for Owen's sake she forced herself to act as normal as possible. Well, other than the constant glancing around the room, looking for anyone suspicious.

A man strolled in through the door to the dining room. His hands were in his pockets, his stance casual, but his dark eyes flitted across the customers, lingering a fraction too long on her and Owen.

A chill rippled across her shoulders.

When Micah returned with three ice cream cones, she tipped her head toward the man, who now stood with his shoulder leaning against the wall.

"What do you think?" she whispered. "Is he an officer?"

He stole a discreet glance in the man's direction before shaking his head. "I don't know, but I don't like the look of him." He pulled out his cell and took a quick glance at the notifications. "Your sister's here."

Abigail's spine sagged in relief. *Thank You, Lord.* Maybe He wasn't listening, maybe it was just habit, but she couldn't help it. Not with Owen still in danger.

"Eat your ice cream quick, honey," she told Owen as he licked a big drop from the side of his cone. "Auntie Eleanor is here." She turned to Micah. "Where should we meet her? Outside?"

He shook his head. "She's already inside, in the section with the kids' toys. That way." He pointed discreetly at the other entrance to the ice cream shop.

She wiped Owen's hands and mouth, then wadded up the napkin and stuffed it into her half-eaten cone. "Okay, let's go."

Micah slung the duffel strap over his shoulder and gathered the trash while she picked up Owen. As she followed him to a waste bin near the door, she glanced back toward where the man had been standing. He wasn't there.

Her heart thumped a little harder. Maybe he'd just slipped into the next shop over…?

No. He was weaving through the line of people in front of the ice cream counter. His hard gaze landed on Abigail, and in that instant she had no doubt she was the intended target.

They'd been found.

* * *

"He's following us," Abigail hissed. Her face had gone deathly pale.

Micah dropped their trash into the garbage can and whipped his head around. The man she'd pointed out a few minutes ago had picked up his pace and was now shoving his way through the crowd, heading straight toward them. It wasn't David or Vincenzo, but his brown hair and stature were a fit for the man who Micah had seen inside Abigail's home.

He pressed a hand against Abigail's back and guided her toward the doorway to the next room. More tourists had piled into the place in the past fifteen minutes, maybe even a tour bus or two judging by the crowd. Could they lose the man in here?

Abigail ducked off to the side, partially shielding herself from view behind a tall rack of mini South Dakota license plates organized by name. "We have to split up," she said. "It's me they're after. You take Owen to my sister, and I'll lead that man away."

She pressed her lips to Owen's hair, then shoved him into Micah's arms.

"Wait, Abigail, it's too—"

Dangerous. The word died on his tongue as she darted around him and up one of the aisles. The brown-haired man entered the room, glancing over the crowd. Micah hugged the wall, ducking and focusing his attention on the license plates like he was looking for a specific name.

"Mommy?" Owen's lips turned down as he watched Abigail walk away. The last thing he needed was for Owen to start screaming for her, or they'd think *he* was a kidnapper.

"She's got something to do while we find Aunt Eleanor," Micah whispered. "But right now, we're going to hide here super quiet."

"Like hide-and-seek? Is Aunt Eleanor looking for us?"

"Sort of. Quiet now."

He held his breath as the man strode past, his heavy boots thumping on the linoleum floor, but he passed by without glancing in Micah's direction. Far across the room, Abigail's ginger hair flashed through the crowd, and she slipped through a doorway in the back. The restrooms? More of the dining room? He wracked his brain but couldn't recall the huge store's layout.

Their pursuer wove through the shoppers heading after her, and as soon as a dozen shoppers stood between them, Micah carried Owen in the other direction. *Lord, please protect Abigail.*

He kept checking over his shoulder as he

passed through the vendor spaces, heading to the farthest edge of the store where they sold candy and kids' toys. Thankfully, Abigail's sister had had the foresight to text a picture of herself, so Micah would know what she looked like.

The front door behind him jangled as he carried Owen past a glass case of turquoise jewelry. He waited until he was partially shielded by a clothing rack to glance back. A man strode into the store, and Micah's gut clenched. The blond hair and amber eyes were instantly recognizable—*David*. That story about him heading back to Chicago had clearly been a ruse to fool the police. Or a lie *told* by the police.

He pressed Owen close and kept low behind the racks as he headed deeper into the huge gift emporium. The best thing he could do right now was get Owen safely to Eleanor. Then he'd be able to find and help Abigail. He paused for a precious moment to fire off a text to Abigail's sister.

They've found us. Be to you in 2.

He glanced back, his gaze accidentally connecting with David's above a huge crowd piling inside from a tour bus out front. Recognition flashed across David's face. Micah didn't wait to see what he'd do—instead, he hugged Owen closer and hustled through the shoppers to the far edge of the store.

With her red hair a few shades brighter than Abigail's, Eleanor was easy to spot among all the jostling families in the crowd. She stood close to the exit on the far side, scanning the room. Worry lined her face, but she brightened as he approached with Owen.

She pressed a hand to her chest. "Thank the Lord, you made it." Then she frowned. "Where's Abigail?"

"She led them in the other direction." He clenched his teeth, then gave Owen a quick squeeze. "Time to go with Aunt Eleanor now, little man. I loved hanging out with you today."

Eleanor took the duffel bag and held out her arms. "Hey, Owen! I'm so excited to see you. I've missed you so much!"

The little boy's eyes twinkled above the thumb in his mouth, and he pushed against Micah's chest, reaching for his aunt. Good. He'd be happy with her until Abigail was safe.

As Eleanor took the child and his bag, Micah glanced back across the crowd. No sign of David, but he could materialize any second. "You'd better go now. Head straight for the car and get out of town. Text if you have any concerns at all. Okay?"

She nodded, her face grim. "Tell my sister to call me as soon as she can." She paused, looking him over. "And please, take care of her. She doesn't have anyone else left."

"I will."

The bell jangled over the glass door as she headed out with Owen. The little boy waved at him over her shoulder, red lobster claws bobbing behind his back, and for a moment, a flash of sadness washed through Micah's chest. Probably caused by the harsh reality of having to separate Owen from his mother. Certainly, it couldn't be because Micah would miss him. He'd only just met the child.

He watched until they were lost to sight, weaving through cars in the busy parking lot. No sign of the pursuers. A slow breath eased out of his chest, and he turned to see David pressing his way through the doorway from the next section over. Pretending he was still carrying Owen, Micah worked his way toward the back, where another door connected into the recesses of the store.

But when he reached the entry and glanced back, David wasn't following him anymore. Instead, he was heading back the way he'd come. Better than following Eleanor and Owen, but...

His chest tightened. Did that mean they'd caught Abigail?

All he could do now was pray he'd get to her in time.

Abigail's breath came in shallow gasps as she roamed through the maze of Wall Drug. The man was still after her. He'd paused once, almost as if shooting off a text, but then he'd been right back on her tail.

And now she was utterly disoriented. How huge was this place?

She'd almost ducked inside the women's restroom when she passed it, but what if there was no exterior window? She'd be trapped, with nowhere left to run.

Maybe a security guard or store clerk could help, but she couldn't go to anyone yet. Not until she'd led her follower on a long enough cat-and-mouse chase to make sure Micah got Owen to Eleanor. She wanted her sister and her little boy long gone before this chase ended.

She blinked away the moisture clouding her vision as she hurried through another section of the dining room, beneath antler chandeliers and past a café counter. She hadn't dared risk glancing back at Owen for one last look. All she'd heard was his small voice carrying after her. *Mommy?* Her throat burned.

But he'd be safe, and that was what mattered.

"Abigail!" a male voice called, and her stomach plunged into her knees. David threaded his way through the tables from another direction, and he had enough of a lead to cut her off. Curious bystanders looked up from their lunches, watching as she turned and hurried through another door leading to a hallway.

The space was almost eerily quiet after the chaos of the rest of the place. Was this for employees only? Could she find someone who might be able to help?

But as she rushed forward, a third man stepped in front of her, cutting off her escape route. Vincenzo. A slow smile crept across his face.

Her heart hammered as she scanned the space for options. Two closed doors—offices, maybe?—and what looked like another open corridor. Could she get to any of them in time?

Just as she was about to lunge for the nearest door, two arms wrapped around her from behind, a hand clapping over her mouth. She kicked and struggled as her attacker hoisted her off the ground, dragging her forward.

"This way." Vincenzo led the way into the corridor, and the other man dragged her after him. At the end, a red emergency exit sign glowed over a big metal door.

"Good, you found her," David said, entering the corridor behind them.

So much for the cops' insistence she wasn't in danger. Had he found Owen too? *Please, God, no!*

She writhed again in the man's grasp, struggling to open her mouth to bite his hand, but his grip was like iron. At least if they were all here, with her, they weren't chasing Owen. She had that consolation.

"Let's end this mess." David pushed past her and strode toward the door. He shoved the heavy door open, revealing a glimpse of blue sky and parking lot outside but also triggering the fire alarm. Loud sirens echoed throughout the space, bouncing off the walls and assaulting her ears. In the distance, the sound of harried voices and thumping footsteps swept through the air.

Now everyone would empty out of this place, and Micah and the security guards would never see these men hauling her off to their vehicle. David walked outside, leaving Vincenzo to hold the door.

But as her assailant dragged her toward the open exit, footsteps pounded behind them.

"Abigail! Let her go!"

Micah? *Thank You, God!*

She twisted again, kicking viciously at the

man's shins. A heavy weight crashed against them, making the man stagger, and she jammed her elbow into his ribs. He grunted, relaxing his arms enough for her to wrench free.

"Abigail, get help!" Micah called as he struggled with the man from behind. Vincenzo had released his hold on the door and was now dashing back inside.

Without looking back, she raced down the corridor and into the café, where frazzled store employees were guiding shoppers toward the exits.

She scanned the area and her gaze landed on a security guard. She rushed up to him. "Help, please, my friend is being attacked!"

His brows pulled together but he nodded toward the woman he'd been directing and hastened after Abigail as she led the way to the back hall.

"This way," she called over the sirens. "The emergency exit."

As they turned into the corridor, she saw Micah swing at Vincenzo, who staggered backward, pressing a hand to his cheek.

The security guard pulled out a Taser and advanced toward the struggling men. "Freeze! Security! Back away from each other and put your hands up where I can see them."

Micah complied immediately, but Vincenzo and the other man exchanged a glance and bolted for the exit, shoving their way out into the parking lot.

The security guard muttered a curse as he pulled out a walkie-talkie and relayed a code into it. Then he turned to Micah. "Hands out. I'm taking you into custody until we figure out what this was all about."

"But he didn't—" Abigail started.

The guard gave her a sharp look as he advanced toward Micah. "Would you like to be cuffed too?"

She shook her head, watching silently as he placed a pair of handcuffs on Micah's wrists. "Now come with me." He led the way toward the door. "We'll have to wait outside until the fire department clears the building."

They stepped out into the hot parking lot, the summer sun beating down on their heads, but at least it was relatively quiet out there. No sign of David or the other two men. They'd vanished into the crowded parking lot, where several shoppers had given up and were getting into their cars. Others stood in clusters outside the store entrances.

"You've got the wrong idea here," Micah said to the guard. "Sheriff Layton should've already advised your team and sent extra units. Those men attacked *us*."

"Sorry, but I have no idea what you're talking about," the guard replied. "You just keep quiet while we wait."

Confusion rippled across Micah's forehead, reflecting how Abigail felt. He'd told her Detective Overton was taking care of everything. Had the chain of communication fallen short somehow? Or had the sheriff decided this operation wasn't worth his time?

"Micah, what about Owen? Did you get him to my sister?" she asked.

"Yes, he's safe." Micah's blue eyes connected with hers, and the care radiating from them momentarily stalled her breath. *Nonsense*. He was just doing his job. Unlike the sheriff.

"Hey, that's enough talking," the guard snapped, jabbing his Taser in Micah's direction.

Another guard ran up from around the side of the building, and the two conferred for a few minutes before calling the sheriff's office. Twenty minutes later, both Micah and Abigail sat in an interview room across from a police officer who introduced himself as Deputy Hansen.

"We need to speak to Sheriff Layton," Micah insisted. "He should've known what we were doing at Wall Drug." He repeated the same explanation he'd given the security guard.

The officer tapped a pen against his notepad. "Well, here's the thing, the sheriff didn't mention any of this to us. I suppose we could contact RCPD to see if Detective Overton backs up your story."

"Can you please ask Layton?" Micah asked.

"Maybe. I can see if he's available."

As the officer stood, Micah held up his still-cuffed hands. "What charges are you holding me under?"

"Assault and battery."

Micah groaned. This was utterly ridiculous. He nodded toward Abigail. "I was defending Abigail and myself."

"That's why we're here, Mr. Ellis." Hansen shrugged. "To determine if charges need to be pressed." He walked over to a phone on the wall and asked for the sheriff, who appeared a few minutes later.

The man's face matched his voice—tanned and leathery after years in the desert. He strolled inside and leaned against the opposite wall, chewing lazily on a piece of gum. "All right, I'm here, Ranger Ellis. Care to explain why you were creating a fracas in my tourist shop? Did you set off the alarm too?"

Heat flashed beneath Micah's skin, but he inhaled and exhaled slowly through his nose.

"No, that would've been David Blakely and his mobster friends. The ones you said returned to Chicago."

The sheriff blinked, then exchanged a look with the deputy, who flashed his notepad as if to say, "Already got it down." The entire conversation would be recorded too.

"Well now, are you sure it was him?" Layton asked.

"Quite." Micah glanced at Abigail, who nodded her agreement.

"Sounds like I'll be needin' to have a chat with Chicago PD about their sources. What were they after?"

"Abigail." He nodded in her direction. "Somehow, they learned we'd be here to hand Abigail's son over to her sister, but it wasn't the boy they were after. They went for her."

How had they known to show up at Wall Drug right then? No one had followed them from Abigail's home, and they'd left her phone in Interior just in case it was being traced. It was *almost* like they'd been tipped off…

"Which brings me to my next point, Sheriff," he went on. "Detective Overton told me you'd have extra officers on patrol just in case something like this happened, but no one was here."

Layton's gray eyebrows bunched together. "He said what now?"

Micah repeated his conversation with Brian, the one in which they'd arranged for the safest possible exchange. Yet, the sheriff's look of confusion remained. It *had* to be an act. Somewhere there was a weak link in the chain, and it wasn't Brian. Not only was Brian his friend, but he was also an excellent cop.

But what reason would the sheriff have to lie?

Finally, the sheriff pushed off from the wall and stood in front of Micah. "I'll check my records. See if someone else here took the call and didn't pass the message to me."

But Brian spoke with you himself. Micah wanted to say it, but he decided not to push, especially in front of Deputy Hansen. The sheriff would only get defensive. Instead, he'd talk to Brian again. See if they could figure out what had happened.

Maybe the sheriff hadn't ever even called Chicago PD. Maybe he'd only made that up as an excuse to pull the patrol car. A knot twisted in his stomach. If the sheriff was on the mob's side, Abigail was in even more danger than he'd thought.

On his way out the door, Layton turned to Hansen. "Get descriptions of the men again, then release him."

Half an hour later, the deputy dropped Micah

and Abigail off at her car in the Wall Drug parking lot. She stared at the storefront for a long moment, as if lost in thoughts about Owen.

He stood next to her, fighting the urge to wrap an arm around her shoulders. Why did the thought of comforting her feel so natural? "He's going to be all right. He was really excited to see your sister."

She nodded, eyes blinking rapidly. "I know." The way her voice quavered tugged painfully at his heart.

Despite his better judgment, he placed a hand on her shoulder and squeezed. Surely a little comfort was all right? After all she'd been through? "Why don't you drive?" he suggested, heading for the passenger side.

When they stopped for a red light on the way out of town, his phone pinged with a text. He held up the picture from Eleanor for Abigail to see. Owen, hugging his stuffed lion and waving from the back seat. The message was short.

Made it to the Wyoming border. We miss you.

Abigail let out a long, shuddering breath. "Good."

"That's a definite answer to prayer." He

watched her, waiting to see how she'd react after what she'd told him about her faith.

"Yeah. It is. Maybe He was listening after all." She cast him a quick glance, her eyebrows quirked up in an expression of hopefulness that was downright cute.

"He always is," he reassured her, then forced his gaze out the window and kept his tone neutral as he directed her onto the interstate heading east. Yes, she was caring, intelligent, and attractive. But Taylor had seemed that way too. And Abigail was the last woman who'd be looking for a relationship any time soon. Not to mention, she had an entire life in another city—or she would as soon as he helped free her from the mob.

When he finally dared to glance back at her again several minutes later, her knuckles had gone white on the steering wheel. Her shoulders were rigid, and she kept glancing at the rearview mirror.

"Abigail? What's up?"

"That car coming up behind me. It looks *very* familiar."

He twisted in his seat to look out the back window. A white sedan swerved out from behind a semi-truck and into Abigail's lane, flying way too fast even for the South Dakota speed limit.

His stomach tightened as he got a good look at the vehicle. It was the car from her street. The mobsters must have been watching the Wall Drug parking lot, waiting for them to return.

And now, from the way that car was barreling toward them, they weren't worried about catching Abigail anymore.

They wanted to kill her.

FIVE

Micah's heart thudded against his ribs as he watched the white car speed closer and closer to the back of Abigail's SUV. This stretch of I-90 had two lanes, but if those orange construction signs up ahead were any indication, they might be down to one any minute. Thankfully the road wasn't crowded, but that could change in an instant. The same amount of time it would take to get killed in a high-speed collision.

"They're going to ram us, aren't they?" Abigail's voice was tight as her gaze darted between the rearview mirror and the road in front of them. She clutched the steering wheel like it was a lifeline. "What do I do?"

The SUV picked up speed as she pressed the accelerator, whether consciously or not, pushing the speedometer close to ninety mph. Vibrations rumbled through the seat beneath his legs. Orange flashed on the side of the road as they flew past the work zone signs. The speed limit here dropped to sixty mph, and for once, he prayed there would be a cop waiting to pull drivers over.

"Our exit is coming up." He pointed ahead to a green sign just visible on the horizon. "Route 240. Maybe we can shake them if you wait till the last second." If not, at least they'd be taking the high-speed chase off the interstate and away from innocent passersby.

Her throat bobbed. "Okay."

"You've got this, Abigail. And your SUV has all-wheel-drive. It'll give you extra traction."

"This isn't where we got on the interstate."

"No," he said. "We're exiting earlier."

The green sign came closer, and now an orange banner slapped across it dashed Micah's hopes for escape.

Exit closed.

Abigail groaned. "Roadwork?"

The SUV suddenly lurched forward as the white sedan bumped them from behind, and Abigail let out a strangled yelp, struggling to keep control of the wheel. He twisted in his seat, watching as the other vehicle eased up slightly to create a narrow gap between them. Probably to give them more momentum on the next attempt.

They might have to take that exit anyway, so long as she could pick a path safely through the construction. The only things out here were grass and prairie dog mounds, and this SUV would manage off-road if necessary.

He prayed it wouldn't come to that.

Ahead, orange cones lined the right shoulder, giving them less room to maneuver. But if he told her to switch lanes, they'd be trapped on the left, unable to attempt an exit.

"They're coming!" She pressed the gas, pushing the arrow on the speedometer above ninety-five. In the distance, a siren wailed, and blue-and-red lights flashed far behind them in the side mirror.

Thank You, God.

"There's a cop car back there. Maybe they'll scare off the driver." He strained to see ahead, to see what the roadwork looked like at the closed exit. Orange cones far ahead blocked the off-ramp, and he could just make out the top of a digger down below the exit, but there was no sign of movement.

He jerked forward as the white car rammed the back of the SUV again, and the scraping of metal screamed through the cab. The SUV swerved wildly, and for a second he feared they might flip, but Abigail managed to keep the vehicle in its lane.

The cop car was gaining, but not fast enough, not with this driver who had a death wish. It'd be a long way to the next exit—nearly another ten miles—too far to make it. He surveyed the orange cones fast approaching on the right. The pavement was still there, at least as far as he could see before the road dropped out of view. But would it be enough? And would the other vehicle follow?

Behind them, the white car dropped back. Then its engine roared as it leaped forward, this time swerving to clip the left side of the SUV and send it out of control.

"Take the exit!" Micah yelled. "Through the cones, now!"

Abigail jerked the wheel to the right, hitting the brakes as the SUV barreled through a pair of cones and flew onto the off-ramp. Behind them, the white sedan just missed clipping the rear bumper. Its brakes screeched as the driver realized what Abigail had done, but the car had already flown past the exit.

Micah exhaled a huff of air, but they weren't safe yet. Up ahead the pavement ended where workers had dug up a giant section of the off-ramp, just before the junction with Route 240. He flew forward against the seat belt as Abigail slammed the brakes, making the tires squeal. Off to the left, closer to the overpass, a crew of construction workers on break watched wide-eyed as the SUV stopped a mere car's length away from the trench.

Her breath came in ragged gasps. She turned to look at him, eyes big and questioning. Were they safe now? Behind them the police siren drew closer.

Up ahead, the white sedan cranked a 180-degree turn and took off down the opposing on-ramp, illegally driving in the wrong direction.

Micah grabbed Abigail's arm. "Go! Go!" He gestured toward the grass on the right side. "Over the grass, get to the road and head south. That way!"

She steered the SUV onto the tough prairie grass. They bounced and jostled across the terrain until the front tires hit asphalt and they were back on the road. As Abigail punched the gas, he tapped in an emergency call and notified the dispatcher of the chase.

Sirens screamed nearby. He twisted in his seat to see the police cruiser barrel down the closed off-ramp. But it wasn't close enough to intercept the other vehicle. The white sedan skidded as the driver reached the bottom of the ramp and turned onto the road behind their SUV. Somewhere farther back, the cruiser bounced over the prairie grass.

But Abigail had accelerated fast enough the interstate was dwindling to a tiny speck in the distance. His phone rang. The dispatcher issued instructions, and he relayed them to Abigail.

"There's another officer ahead in six miles. He's got a spike strip set up across the road. It was too risky to try to lay it after we pass." Which meant Abigail's tires would deflate too.

She cast a worried glance his direction. "What if they have guns?"

"We'll keep you safe. The other officer is following us, so there'll be two cruisers. If they can arrest these guys, that could give us some real help in tracking down who else might be after you."

Her knuckles stayed white on the steering wheel, but she nodded. Then she glanced in the rearview mirror and stiffened. "They're almost caught up to us. Should I speed up? Or will I lose control of the car when I hit the spikes?"

"No, they don't cause a blowout. Instead, it'll take fifteen to twenty seconds for the tires to deflate. You can speed up."

He slipped a hand through the grab handle above the inside of the passenger side door as she pressed the gas. The car was pushing ninety mph again, dangerously fast for this two-lane road. Small rocks and debris on the asphalt clattered up against the undercarriage and went shooting out sideways.

Something clanged against the SUV's tailgate, sending a jolt of adrenaline through his system. That wasn't a rock.

"What was that?" Abigail's neck and shoulders were so rigid she could've been carved from stone.

He twisted in his seat. The sun glinted off something propped outside the passenger side window.

"Duck!" he called, hunching his shoulders to drop his head behind the seat's headrest as Abigail did the same. "They're firing at us!"

More bullets bit into the back of the vehicle, and Abigail shrieked as glass shattered. Micah drew his handgun from his shoulder holster and aimed it out the open window, firing at the front of the car tailing them. The passenger's gun pulled back in, and the car slowed, creating a bigger gap between them.

"I see the cop car ahead." She eased off the gas as they approached the cruiser. The white car started to gain on them again, but in a moment it would be too late.

Micah swiveled back around to the front. The spike strip lay like a straight black snake across the road. "Steady."

She nodded tensely. Then they were flying over the spikes. All four tires hissed as the air leaked out, and the SUV's dashboard lit up with warnings as the tire pressure dropped. Behind them, the white sedan tried to brake, but it was too late.

"Let the car roll to a stop," Micah said. "Don't hit the brakes or they'll rear-end us." Might try it anyway, but that couldn't be helped now.

The other police cruiser, the one behind them, slowed to a near stop and then drove around the strip off-road. Abigail let the SUV keep rolling until the tires deflated. Behind them, the driver of the white sedan tried to force his vehicle forward, but the vehicle's smaller tires deflated faster than the SUV's and he was forced to stop thirty yards back.

The two police cars, with sirens and lights on, pulled up on either side, blocking the road.

"Stay down," Micah ordered, and Abigail ducked low in her seat. Sweat beaded on her pale forehead.

He opened the passenger door and stepped

out, gun at the ready, but no one moved inside the white car. One of the police officers climbed out of his cruiser, standing behind the cover of the open driver's door, and called, "Get out of the vehicle and put your hands on your head."

Micah held his breath as he waited. Would the men comply?

After a tense moment, both front doors of the vehicle opened, and the two men got out, hands on their heads. In a matter of minutes, the officers had them handcuffed and in the back of one of the cruisers.

Micah stowed his gun back into its holster and turned to Abigail, who was still crouched in the driver's seat. "They've been arrested. It's over."

At his words, the tension drained out of Abigail's body in a flood, leaving her hands shaking. Tears sprang to her eyes and she swallowed, desperately trying to keep them back. The last thing she wanted was to fall apart in front of Micah, but between the attack at the store and that high-speed chase...

"Oh, Abigail. It's okay. You're all right." Micah's gentle words tore at the wall she was trying to build, and the tears burst loose.

She swiped at her cheeks as he walked

around the front of the car and pulled her door open.

"Come here." He helped her out of the car, and before she knew it, he'd enfolded her in his strong arms. For a moment the rest of the world vanished, and she leaned into the comfort and protection of his embrace, like a barricade blocking out all the bad things trying to hurt her. When was the last time she'd felt this safe? Or trusted someone on this instinctive, heart level?

She inhaled deeply, the first full breath she felt like she'd taken in weeks. Owen was safe, and for a moment, she was too. Cool evergreen wrapped around her senses like a soothing balm for her tattered soul, so different from the spicy cologne Eric had favored.

Eric. Acid rose in her stomach. She'd trusted him too, hadn't she? Enough to marry him. And look how *that* had turned out.

No, with her track record, she couldn't risk getting close to a man again. No matter how caring and protective he seemed.

She took a deep breath and pushed away from Micah's chest, wiping away the last of the tears as he released her. "Thank you. I wasn't sure we were going to make it for a minute there."

Emotion flickered in his blue eyes, but he

stuffed his hands in his pockets and stepped back. "Me either, but God was looking out for us." When one of the officers approached them, Micah turned away from her and headed toward him.

Taking a steadying breath, she straightened her spine and followed a minute later.

"Hey," Micah said when she joined them, "if you're up to it, we'll need to head back to Wall to identify the two suspects."

"Yes, of course." That was one silver lining to the terrifying car chase—they'd arrested the two men. As she watched, the police cruiser carrying the suspects turned around on the narrow road and headed north. Both their vehicle and hers looked forlorn and abandoned resting on their rims. "What about my car?"

The police officer held out his hand and she shook it. "Officer Pettison. Dispatch has a tow truck on the way to pick up both vehicles. There's a tire place in Wall. You can get a ride with me, and hopefully your vehicle will be ready by the time we're done at the station."

She smiled gratefully.

An hour passed by the time they waited for the tow truck and then rolled back into Wall. Hard to believe they'd pulled in here with Owen only this morning. Maybe all the action was a good thing—it helped keep her mind off what she'd temporarily lost.

Micah nudged her arm. "Getting sick of this town yet?"

"Maybe a bit." She laughed as they passed a huge sign for Wall Drug on the way to the station. "It's a little different than Chicago."

"Do you miss it? The city?" He squinted under the sun's glare. "Maybe I shouldn't ask, given the circumstances."

"It's okay." She tapped her fingers lightly against the car door. "You know, I loved all the opportunities and things to do, and I do miss my house. A few friends. But mostly…"

The words trailed away as she tried to figure out exactly what she wanted to say. *Did* she miss Chicago? Not really, if she was being honest. Life there had been so intertwined with Eric and their struggling relationship. They'd had their good moments, but so much of their life together had been…*work.* A daily grind to create peace instead of conflict when they were so different, to take care of Owen alone while Eric worked long hours, to reconcile her growing sense of regret with the vows she'd made. The counselor they'd seen for a few sessions reminded her that godly marriages were more about holiness than happiness, but she couldn't help wishing happiness didn't feel so far out of reach. It was hard to look back on that time of her life positively.

As awful as the last few months had been, something about being here felt like—she was almost hesitant to admit it—a fresh start. Like there might be unexpected freedom on the other side of the trauma.

The thought caught her off guard. Freedom? Was that what had defined her relationship with Eric? The sense of being trapped?

She glanced at Micah. He was watching her, his blue gaze speculative, as if trying to read the thoughts tracking through her mind. His focused attention sent a little thrill through her system but triggered all the alarms in her brain at the same time. If the whole point of starting over was to gain freedom, why in the world would she ever consider another relationship?

Ridiculous. He wasn't thinking anything of the sort.

"It's more beautiful out here in the desert than I expected," she finished, breaking eye contact with him to watch out the front window as the officer pulled into the station's parking lot. That was safe to say, wasn't it? "Even though Eleanor lives in Wyoming, I've only been out to visit her a few times. We always flew."

The officer cut the engine and they got out of the car. Perfect timing, considering these personal conversations with Micah would lead to nowhere good.

"You two sure like my station." Sheriff Layton glanced up from a stack of papers as Officer Pettison ushered them down a hallway.

"We'd prefer not to visit again." Micah's tone oozed false politeness that matched his fake smile, and Abigail couldn't stop her lips from turning up. It was nice to have someone else on her team, someone who understood law enforcement.

Pettison opened the door to a room overlooking a lineup of men of varying heights and shades of brown hair, all wearing surly expressions. "I know you might not have gotten a good look at them, but we'd like to see if you can identify the men who were chasing you, Ms. Fox."

The driver was easy to pick out from the others—his face might stay etched in her mind forever. She pointed to him. "He's the one who was driving today and the day they broke into my house. But the other man—" she chewed her lip "—I'm not sure. I don't want to pick the wrong person."

"Ranger Ellis?"

Micah, who had been leaning against the wall, pushed forward and pointed toward a shorter, dark-haired man. "Him. He was inside her house."

Pettison nodded. "Thanks. He was the passenger today. We figured he was part of the break-in too but needed your confirmation. I'll get them processed while Layton asks you a few questions."

A few minutes later, Abigail took a seat in one of the uncomfortable interview chairs next to Micah and waited for the sheriff. It didn't take long to go over what had happened. The sheriff took notes, frowning occasionally, then said, "Good thing my officers were close at hand."

Micah exchanged a glance with her but nodded. "Yes, it was. Truly providential." Did he suspect Layton of failing to help earlier on purpose? "I'd like to listen in when you interrogate the men."

Layton shook his head. "I'm afraid that won't be possible."

Micah stiffened. "Detective Overton, then?"

"Not his jurisdiction, as these men weren't involved in the kidnapping." Layton tapped his pen against the table lazily, almost as if he was enjoying Micah's irritation. Then he straightened. "But the real issue is that both men have already claimed their Miranda rights, so none of us will be hearing from them until they have lawyers."

"What about the Chicago PD? Did you contact them to get the faces run through their database?" Micah asked.

The sheriff's mouth turned down at the corners, like he was annoyed Micah was telling him how to do his job. Without answering, he stood and tucked his pen back into his pocket. "Thanks for your time, Ranger Ellis. Ms. Fox. I'll be in touch as soon as we have any more information."

Half an hour later, as they sat inside the stuffy waiting area of the tire shop eating room-temperature subs from the sandwich place next door, Micah leaned toward her. "I'm sorry, Abigail. There's something up with that man."

She glanced at the store clerk, who was engaged in a phone call, then looked back at Micah and kept her voice low. "The sheriff? Do you think David or one of the others got to him?"

"I can't think of any other explanation. I get being surly about not wanting other cops stepping on your toes, but…" He shook his head. "First he pulls the patrol on your street, then he doesn't send any extra officers for our planned exchange of Owen, and now this complete lack of helpfulness. I don't like it."

Could the mob have gotten to the cops here?

Something clenched inside her chest, like a screw being overtightened until it was about to snap. "There's nowhere I'll ever be safe, is there?" She picked at her stale sandwich bread. "And Owen. How will I ever be able to get him back? Should I ask to be put in witness protection?"

Micah swallowed a mouthful of food. "No, you don't want to do that. Not yet. If you vanish, we'll never get your husband's evidence into the right hands. That's how we're going to end this mess. When we get back to Interior, I'm calling Chicago PD myself to see if I can get some answers."

"But I've already taken you away from so much of your work. Won't you get in trouble?" Guilt fought with the gratitude warming her insides. How could she ask him to keep helping her? Especially when his life had been put on the line this afternoon too?

The intensity in his gaze made her stomach flutter. "Don't you worry about me, Abigail. I'll be just fine. All that matters is helping *you*."

He'd said that to her a lot in their short

acquaintance—so giving and concerned, so willing to sacrifice. But nobody had a perfect life. He must have needs and concerns of his own. What was his story? Why was he living out here all alone?

She was supposed to be keeping him at arm's length, not looking for ways to get more involved in his life. The answers to those questions shouldn't matter.

Then why did telling herself this fact make no difference?

It was late by the time they made it back to Interior. The end to one long, exhausting day. Abigail had borne up under the strain admirably, smiling through her tears when they received word from Eleanor that she'd made it home with Owen. But she'd gone back to wringing her hands again as they drove, when she thought he wasn't looking. She'd asked him to drive, which was understandable given the trauma of the car chase.

"What is it?" he asked finally as he turned onto her street.

"I… I'm sorry," she began, glancing at him. "I know I shouldn't worry since the officer is here, but… David must know where I live by now. I'm not sure how I can sleep here. Should I find a hotel?"

She had a good point. An officer out front wouldn't prevent someone from sneaking in the back.

"Not a hotel. There's nothing out here, and they'd find a way to track you." He pulled into her driveway. "If you're up for it, why don't you come with me back to Ben Reifel? You can take a nap on the couch in our break room while I make some calls. I work with some amazing women—I'm sure one of them would take you in for a couple of days until we decide what to do next."

Abigail's face cleared. "Okay, let's do that. I'll run in and grab a bag."

When she returned a few minutes later, her expression had clouded over again. "What about the officer? If we tell him where I'm going, will word get back to Sheriff Layton?"

"Yeah, that could be a problem." Micah sucked on his lower lip. If the mob *had* gotten to Layton, they needed to keep Abigail's whereabouts secret. But he could hardly go tell the officer to head home. "For right now, I'll tell him the truth—that I'm taking you into the park with me for the evening. After that, we'll figure it out."

By the time they pulled into the Ben Reifel headquarters parking lot, the last rays of burning sunlight streaked from behind the buttes to the west. Pink and purple cloud ribbons gleamed against the fading blue sky, and the earth below glowed in shades of orange. The familiar scents of sand and dry heat felt as much like home as the grit of dust beneath his feet. Whatever uncertainties, whatever heartaches life brought, being out here in the peaceful desert always helped him heal. He loved it here. As he drew near the building's entrance, he glanced back to see Abigail standing on the sidewalk, staring at the sunset.

"Spectacular, isn't it?" he asked.

She nodded, taking a few steps toward him with her focus still on the sky. "I've never seen anything like it. It looks like something out of a postcard. Like God reached down and painted those mountains Himself."

"I like that." A smile played at his lips. Maybe all the awful things that had happened would help lead her back to the Lord. "Do you know why the native peoples called this area the Badlands?"

"Hard to imagine, with sunsets like this. Was it because it's so dry, and there's nothing to drink?"

"No, it was because the terrain is hard to cross. All the buttes and sand make it too rugged for easy movement." He nodded toward the golden west. "But the sunsets are gorgeous."

Like her, actually. The thought caught him off guard, but it was true. Any man with eyes in his head would think the same thing. Her green irises shone brightly in the fading light, and the faintest trace of freckles danced across her petite nose.

She smiled, tucking a strand of coppery hair behind her ear, then cleared her throat. "Is that why you wanted to work for the park service? The sunsets?"

"They do say that's how we get paid." He chuckled. If only it were truly that simple, but Abigail didn't need to hear his sob story. They had an investigation to tackle. He turned for the building and she tailed after him.

"Seriously, though," she said as he stopped in front of the door. "Did you always want to be a ranger?"

She wanted to hear more? Funny, most people took his career choice at face value and didn't ask questions. Maybe the badge scared them away.

"No. When I was a kid, I wanted to be a pilot like my dad. He used to fly Cessnas, doing supply drops and taking tourists up. Ran a flight school for a while." He fiddled with the key ring, looking for the right key and avoiding eye contact. It wasn't a great story to tell—veered too much into pity territory. Hopefully, she'd let it go.

"That explains the model airplanes."

He glanced up, brows quirking. "You mean in my living room?"

"And the book on your coffee table about the history of airplanes. It looked older."

So much for hoping. "My mom gave it to me for my eighth birthday. When she left…" He shrugged. "I blamed my dad. Didn't want anything to do with him or his career for years. He quit flying soon after anyway." The memory burned deep inside, searing his conscience. How painful that must've been for his father, absorbing all the unwarranted anger of a hurt little boy on top of his own heartache.

Why was he dumping all this on her anyway? It'd taken four months of dating before he'd told Taylor any of it. Abigail was far too easy to confide in. He found the right key and stuffed it into the lock, grateful for an excuse not to look at her.

"I'm so sorry, Micah." Her fingers grazed his elbow, light as a butterfly's wings.

He swallowed, then turned to face her. The ache in her eyes matched the way he felt. She knew all about broken relationships, didn't she? Somehow that sense of solidarity eased some of the old hurt torquing his insides. "It worked out better like this anyway. I get to do two of my favorite things—help people and spend time outdoors. I couldn't ask for much more."

"And you make the models as a hobby?"

"I picked it up a few years ago, as a way to reconnect with my dad." He turned the key and held the door open. "We work on a new one whenever we get together."

"That's a really neat idea." She smiled as she walked past him, and he couldn't help wondering if he'd just opened a metaphorical door better left shut. Sharing with someone you needed to keep at arm's length was *not* a smart plan. Better to focus on why they were here.

Headquarters was empty at this hour, so he led the way through the darkened Visitor Center and flipped on lights in the rangers' workspace in the back. "There's a couch in here," he said, opening the door to a small break room off the main hallway. "You can get a little rest while I make the phone calls. I can find some change if you want anything." He tipped his head toward the vending machine glowing like an alien spaceship in the corner. The thing was always half-empty, and he suspected the unpopular items had to be well past their expiration dates.

She glanced at it and shook her head. "No thanks, I'm good."

"Probably a wise choice." He threw a thumb in the direction of his desk. "I'll be just down the hall if you need anything."

"Thanks, Micah. I really appreciate it."

He left her settling in on the couch—a green vinyl-clad monstrosity that reminded him of the furniture version of a dinosaur—and went to his desk. He called Brian Overton first, even though he hated disturbing his friend at home.

"Their names are Franco Rossi and Justin Weinstein," Brian told him after he asked about the two suspects. "Layton wouldn't even give you that?"

"No," Micah said, jotting down the names, "but I don't know whether he'd identified them at that point. He did say they claimed their Miranda rights. Do you have anything else on them?"

"Not much. Weinstein owned a vehicle repair shop in Chicago but was indicted for theft of auto parts three years ago. Got out after only two years plus a fine. We don't have anything concrete on Rossi, but he's suspected of mob connections. Want me to send what I've got?" Brian asked.

"Yeah, thanks. Is it worth calling that Chicago officer? Bernetto?"

"You could try, but I don't think he'll have much. Didn't tell me much, at any rate. Other than that story about the mob deciding to let Abigail go."

"Did he believe it? Or has the mob gotten to him?" He rubbed his hand across his forehead. Not knowing who they could trust was the worst part of this case.

"He sounded convinced. His source must've been unreliable." Brian paused, then made a swallowing sound like he'd taken a drink. "Listen, Micah, is there a way to help Abigail find what they want? I think that's the only way to end this, to find the evidence and lock them up. No matter how many individuals we catch, there'll always be more unless we can bring down the boss."

A soft thump sounded somewhere in the distance, barely audible behind Brian's words. Micah swiveled in his chair, glancing toward the hall where Abigail was resting, but she didn't appear. Had she dropped something?

"I agree," he said, scanning the room again. Nothing. "Now that her little boy is safe, I'm planning on taking a couple of days off to head to Chicago with her and see what we can find. Not sure I should trust the cops out there though."

The hairs stood up on his arms, but the room was still and silent. Maybe the events of the last few days were getting to him.

"You can always bring the evidence back here—" Brian's voice cracked, and he cleared his throat. The late nights must be taking their toll. "I've got a local FBI contact I trust. I can arrange a meeting."

"Bypass Layton completely?"

"Exactly. It's not his jurisdiction anyway." Brian chuckled, and Micah laughed with him.

Until a breeze tickled the back of his neck.

He swiveled in the chair. On the far side of the room, past the other rangers' desks, one of the exterior windows had been jimmied open a couple of inches. Night had descended in the last hour, and now it was completely dark outside. Had someone left it like that earlier in the day? The air conditioning in this old building wasn't great. Maybe one of the rangers had propped the window open earlier and forgotten to shut it?

Even as the thought passed through his mind, he knew it wasn't likely. Better to check it out, especially with Abigail asleep in the other room.

"Hey, man, I have to go," he said softly into the phone.

"Wait, do you want—" Brian began, but Micah cut him off.

"Talk later." He hung up the receiver and turned slowly in his chair, hand reaching for the gun in its holster.

Before he could draw it, movement flashed at the window, barely visible against the dark exterior. But the light glinting off the shape resting on the windowsill made the object unmistakable.

The barrel of a gun. And it was aiming directly at him.

SIX

Abigail shifted on the rock-hard vinyl couch, an obvious relic of poor decorating choices from several decades ago. For a second, a longing for home hit her like a tsunami— her leather furniture with the cream-colored throw pillows that had been so hard to keep clean once Owen was born, the exposed wood beams of their ceiling, even the annoying way Eric had insisted the shoes be organized just so in the entryway. Oh, for life to be normal again. Safe and predictable and familiar.

In the blink of an eye, it had all been stripped away. *Why, God?* The prayer went unanswered. Again.

Bitterness clogged her throat and tears sprang into her eyes. But then a thump from the next room made her bolt upright. The pity party vanished in a flash.

What was Micah doing?

She stood, then crept toward the door, her heart pounding double-time.

A sharp crack split the quiet night, then another and another. *Gunshot.* She wanted to scream but managed to clap a hand over her mouth instead as she ducked against the nearest wall. Cold cinderblock iced her back. The shooter wasn't firing into this room—the noise was coming from down the hall.

She stole a glance out into the hall, but all she could see from this vantage point were a few empty desks. *Please, God, keep him safe!* The prayer flew through her mind on instinct, even though she had no reason to expect God would listen this time.

Crashing sounds came from the other room. She had to do something. Abigail slunk out into the hall, keeping low against the wall. Maybe staying hidden would be safer, but she couldn't leave Micah out there all alone. Though, how she could possibly help him, she had no idea. She'd solve that problem when she got to it.

More shots fired, shattering something in a cascade of glass. A window? She pressed her hands to her ears. Her breath came far too quickly, and she forced herself to calm down as she crept closer to the end of the hall. Then suddenly Micah was scrambling across the linoleum floor toward her, ducking from desk to desk. Bullets bit into the desktops, splintering the wood and creating a tornado of loose papers.

"Stay back!" He gestured her away from the open workspace. Not that she had any intention of crawling out into gunfire.

"Is there only one?" she whispered as he crouched next to her.

"I think so, but there could be a driver out in the parking lot."

The gunfire ceased. She huddled closer, as if she could soak up some of his warmth and strength by osmosis.

"Now what?" They couldn't try to leave, could they? Not with an active shooter outside. Surely it was safer inside the building, but in here they were sitting ducks.

Instead of answering, Micah crept back to the edge of the hall and glanced around the corner at the bank of windows across the back wall. No answering fire.

"Is he gone?"

"I doubt it," he said grimly.

As if to punctuate his words, a window rattled open loudly against its frame. A second later, something shattered against the floor in the big open room. Golden light flickered against the desks and the walls, and the smell of smoke hit her senses at the same moment realization struck.

The shooter had started a fire.

Her eyes met Micah's. He shoved his phone into her hands. "Call 911 and stay here. I'll see if I can put it out."

"Be careful!" she called after him, then punched the button for the emergency dispatch. Up above, fire alarms went off. She had to shout over the screeching for the dispatcher to hear her. After relaying their information, she hung up and crept closer to the room where Micah was, pulling her cotton shirt over her mouth.

Black smoke drifted across the ceiling. Micah held a fire extinguisher and was spraying white foam across one of the desks, but they must've used lighter fluid or some other conflagrant, because the blaze was quickly spreading out of control. Above his head, the fire sprinklers in the ceiling came on with a sharp hiss, but the blaze beneath was already consuming the desks faster than the water could cool it. Too little, too late.

"Micah, come on!" she called. "You can't stop it!"

He glanced back at her, then sprayed a few more seconds until the extinguisher ran out. He tossed it aside and ran back to her, coughing. Black film coated his forehead and hairline. Wrapping his hand around hers, he pulled her toward the front of the building. "Let's get out of here!"

The interior lights cut out and emergency lighting kicked on, flashing in white bursts that matched the screech of the alarm. They raced past the information desk, around a diorama of desert animals, and toward the front door of the Visitor Center.

Sparks burst behind one of the big windows at the front, followed by the rapid pelting of gunfire, and Micah shoved Abigail to the ground as the glass shattered in a deadly diamond rain shower. She hit the linoleum hard, hands and chest taking the brunt of the impact, knocking the air out of her lungs.

"Back," he said, his breath warm against her cheek as he crouched between her and the window, shielding her with his body as more shots echoed through the room. "Stay down and keep your shirt over your nose."

On her hands and knees, she raced back the way they'd come. Smoke bit at her throat and eyes, and she blinked rapidly, trying to see. Her hands were coated in dirt and debris as she felt along the edge of the wall for the hallway. Finding it, she said, "Can we get out back here?"

"Yes," he rasped, "there's another door at the end of the hall."

She led the way, keeping low to avoid the smoke, fumbling her way forward as fast as she could crawl. "The dispatcher said fifteen minutes. Where's the fire department? Interior?" The last word caught in her dry throat, and she coughed violently, gasping for air. How had this place filled up with smoke so quickly? How many minutes had it been?

"Interior. They're volunteers." He coughed, a horrible wheezy sound, and she turned back to him in alarm. He'd breathed in far more smoke than she had, trying to battle the blaze. "The NPS...doesn't...have one," he choked out.

"Come on, we have to get you to air." Her too. In the last minute, she'd had to dip her head even closer to the floor to draw in a decent breath. They needed to get to that door. The room with the couch had no exterior access, so she kept crawling past its doorway, moving farther down the hall. Micah said there was a door—was that it, at the far end? A silver bar gleamed intermittently in the flashing lights like a lighthouse leading them to safety.

"Almost there," she said to Micah. When he didn't respond, she turned back to see that he was still crawling after her, but noticeably slower. One hand inching forward at a time, but his breathing came in ragged gasps.

He needed air. Now. Ignoring the burning in her lungs, she forced her aching body forward until her hands hit the hard metal of the door. She shoved against it with all her strength, waiting for the first breath of fresh air, but—

It didn't budge.

No. She reached up, fingers grasping for the metal bar. Maybe she had to push in the right place. Dragging herself upward, she leaned her hip against the bar, but still the door refused to open. Their attacker must have blocked it from the outside.

They were trapped.

She turned, eyes smarting with smoke, and slid down to the floor. Flames licked up the walls at the other end of the hall, searching the cinderblock for anything that would burn. Soon the flames would catch hold of the ceiling and ripple across it, snagging onto the wooden interior doors and door frames and furniture.

Micah lay a few feet away on the floor, far too still. She had to get him to air, find a window to break open, but her lungs burned like they were on fire too, and darkness fogged the edges of her vision.

Why, God? Why did You let this happen to us? Do You hate *me?* The words ripped from her chest like someone had yanked them out of her heart with a fishing hook. Even if she and Eric had deserved God's wrath, Micah didn't.

Or Owen.

His sweet little face appeared before her, making her throat burn with tears that wouldn't come. He'd be an orphan.

Hadn't God promised in His Word never to leave or forsake her? So much for His promises. But was it any more than she should've expected, after everything that had happened?

She slumped to the ground, pressing her cheek against the still-cold linoleum, waiting for the heat to get to their end of the hall. In the silence, she listened, daring God to answer. But He wouldn't have an answer, would He?

Then far away, as if happening in a dream, a familiar sound reached her ears. Not God's voice coming from the flames as He'd spoken to Moses, or a gentle whisper as He'd used with Elijah, but sirens. The earsplitting wail of a fire truck. Maybe more than one.

Help. Help was coming.

Adrenaline surged through her fatigued

muscles, and she pressed her face close to the edge of the door, hoping to catch a breath of fresh air from the outside. Making it to a window wasn't going to happen, not with her legs and arms filled with lead, but she *could* let them know where to look.

The sirens had grown so loud they sounded like they were in the parking lot now. As soon as the noise cut off, she banged on the metal door. First with her fist, then when it hurt too much, she rotated on her back to kick with her feet.

Every movement ached. Her legs had turned into barbells, and the smoke was so low now she could barely draw in enough air even here on the floor. *One more kick, just one more*, she told herself over and over as she fought off the blackness creeping across her vision.

Then something clanged against the outside of the door, and it yanked open in a glorious rush of fresh air and stars glittering like jewels in a velvet sky.

"Survivors here!" a woman shouted. Shadows obscured the stars as figures moved in the doorway.

Arms reached down around her, tugging her outside into the cool desert night. She greedily gasped in one lungful of air after another. Each breath burned, but she was alive.

What about Micah? Panic engulfed her already painful chest and she twisted in her rescuer's arms, trying to see where he was.

"Micah?" She tried to lick her lips, but there was no moisture left in her mouth. "He's…back there…"

"We've got him, miss," said one of the firefighters as they carried her away from the building and helped her sit on the curb at the edge of the parking lot. "Wall Fire and Ambulance will be here any minute. Is anyone else inside?"

"No," she croaked.

The smaller firefighter, a woman, pressed a bottle of water into Abigail's hand. "Try to drink."

She coughed, then held the bottle to her cracked lips. Cool liquid slid against her tongue, easing some of the fiery pain and strengthening her weary body. Two fire trucks had pulled into the lot. Beyond their flashing lights, the roof of the Visitor Center glowed orange against the backdrop of the dark sky. Rushing water shot from one of their hoses toward the blaze. Firefighters called to each other, breaking the surrounding stillness of the desert night, and the air was full of the acrid smell of smoke.

Another pair brought Micah and laid him

down on an emergency blanket on the prairie grass at the edge of the curb. Abigail's heart twisted at the sight of his prone form, but the steady rise and fall of his chest brought a measure of comfort. He curled onto his side, hacking violently, then rolled back again.

Tears stung her eyes. She blinked, but they streamed down her cheeks anyway. Micah had nearly died, and it was all her fault. Who knew what long-term effects he might suffer from the smoke exposure? She should *never* have involved him in this mess.

"Hey..." His voice sounded even worse than hers, and her heart skipped in her chest. He stretched an arm toward her, and she wrapped her fingers around his, so warm and real beneath her grip. If he'd died...

A sob built in her chest. It would've been all her fault.

"Micah—" She swallowed the lump in her throat.

"Now... I know what...it feels like...to be a hot dog," he gasped.

She laughed, swiping at her wet cheeks. Only he would make a joke at a time like this. A cough rattled her rib cage, and she took another drink of water.

One of the first responders knelt next to Micah, offering him a drink too. "You're lucky to be alive. If we hadn't heard pounding on the door and had to search the place instead, you two wouldn't have made it."

Micah squeezed her fingers. His thumb rubbed gently across her knuckles, making her heart twist. This caring, giving, faithful, and kind man was voluntarily helping her and she'd nearly gotten him killed. He shouldn't be in this situation, mixed up with her, and yet... There was no denying how much she appreciated his help and protection. But it went beyond that, didn't it? Almost like there was an invisible cord tugging them together. The thought soothed and terrified her at the same time.

Sirens wailed faintly in the distance. A white SUV with an NPS arrowhead logo on its side pulled into the lot first. The driver parked and got out, then jogged over to where she and Micah waited.

"Micah," he called, "you okay?"

One of the firefighters intercepted the man, who was dressed in jeans and an NPS T-shirt. They spoke in low tones, then the man crouched next to Abigail and offered his hand. "Ms. Fox, I'm Nick Langston, chief ranger for Badlands National Park."

She withdrew her fingers from Micah's and shook his hand. "Nice to meet you."

"I'm glad you're all right, ma'am," he said, then turned to Micah. "As for you, Ranger Ellis, if you ever try to burn down my building again, you'll be looking for a new job."

Micah laughed, then tilted his head to one side, coughing. "Better get those sprinkler heads serviced, Chief."

More approaching sirens cut loudly through the night, and red-and-blue flashing lights appeared around the front of the building as more emergency vehicles turned into the parking lot. Fire trucks, at least one police cruiser, and an ambulance.

Ranger Langston glanced between her and Micah. "Looks like your ride is here. We'll go over the report once you're feeling up to it, and then you're taking a few days off. Got it? And yes, we will definitely update that sprinkler system."

Micah grunted a response and Langston stood, then walked over to join the newly arrived police officers. Firefighters directed the EMTs toward Abigail and Micah. The orange haze over the building's roof was mostly gone, and the fire appeared to be under control. Hopefully, the damage wouldn't be too terrible to the building.

But as the EMTs secured Micah to a stretcher and helped Abigail into the back of the ambulance next to him, a growing sense of resolve hardened in the pit of her stomach. She couldn't let something like this happen to him again. He'd never deserved to get pulled into her problems, and she would *not* let him die because of her.

There was only one thing to do, no matter how terrifying it was. She had to go back to Chicago alone.

Micah's lungs felt like they'd been charred to a blackened crisp on the grill. Come to think of it, so did the inside of his nose, his sinuses, and his throat.

"Next time, leave the firefighting to the professionals," chided the nurse, an older woman with graying hair, as she checked the fluid levels in his IV bag. She fixed him with the stern look he imagined mothers gave their children.

He tugged the oxygen mask down below his mouth. "Interior only has volunteers."

She pursed her lips, frowning at him, until he smiled. Then she shook her head. "Get that mask back up over your face. You've got at least one more hour of oxygen if you want any chance of getting out of here soon."

Obediently he raised the plastic mask back into place, then saluted as she left the room.

He'd already been lying here for ages, with no word from Abigail or anyone else. She wouldn't leave the ER without him, and she'd be safe here. But he didn't like not knowing where she was.

He shifted in the bed, then stared at the clock on the wall as the red second hand ticked around in perfectly rhythmic circles. He *really* didn't like it. The strength of that feeling caught him off guard. Must be because this case was so different from anything he normally handled for the park service. Those were all one-and-done incidents—flat tire, snake sighting, campground infractions. He'd intervene, handle the situation, and never see the person again.

But Abigail—he'd invested a lot into her and Owen, so wasn't it natural he'd feel more strongly about her? About the outcome of the case?

Of course, it was. That explanation made perfect sense. This feeling had nothing to do with the growing attachment between them. Or the fact he felt safer with her than with anyone he'd been around in a long time. There was something about her open, easy manner, her warm thoughtfulness, that drew him right in. Made him *want* to be vulnerable.

But he couldn't let that happen.

He'd poured everything into his relationship with Taylor. Not only financially, but also emotionally, opening his heart and life to her, building plans for their future as things progressed. When he found out she wasn't on the same page—not even in the same *library*—it had crushed him.

Or perhaps it was more accurate to say it had crushed his dream that relationships didn't have to end in heartache the way his parents' marriage had. Because as much as he'd wanted things to work out with Taylor, deep down he knew it was a good thing they hadn't gotten married, not when she wasn't in love with him.

When the doctor finally okayed removing the oxygen an hour later, he was ready to burst out of the hospital bed. But the nurse shook her head. "Don't even think about it. We have to keep you a little longer to make sure you're okay without the oxygen. Things can deteriorate quickly, and we don't want you passing out on the way home."

"Can you tell me what happened to Abigail Fox?" His voice sounded unnaturally raspy, and he cleared his throat. "The woman they brought in with me?"

"Micah?" Abigail's voice came from the doorway behind the nurse, and Micah slumped back on the bed as relief made his spine sag. Even though he knew she wouldn't leave, still...

The nurse raised an eyebrow and smiled as she glanced between the two of them.

It's not like that, he wanted to interject, but she picked up the clipboard and headed for the door.

"I'll leave you two to catch up," she said. "Just go easy on the talking, okay? You need time to heal."

"Hey, how are you doing?" Abigail slipped into the chair next to him and took his hand. Her soft fingers caressed the rough skin on his knuckles, and the concern lining her green eyes made his breath catch. Was it possible... *she* cared about him?

But just as quickly, she let go and broke eye contact, surveying the IV drip and the rest of the room. He must have imagined it. Or read too much into a normal human being's level of concern for someone else. They *had* just been through a near-death experience together. And hadn't his experience with Taylor taught him he was terrible at reading people?

"I'm hanging in there. Thanks to you." He stretched the hand she'd just been holding. Some foolish part of him wished she'd wrap her fingers around it again. "How are *you*? That was close."

Liquid lined her eyes, and she stared down at her hands folded in her lap. "I... I'm so sorry, Micah. You could have died, and it was all my fault."

"It was *not* your fault." He shifted in the bed, angling his body toward her and ignoring the protests of his aching lungs. "Those men chasing you? They're the ones at fault. You did nothing to deserve this." He reached out, but she pressed her hands to her cheeks.

"Neither did you. We didn't tell anyone where we were going. The only reason they would've showed up where you work is if they're targeting *you* now too. I should never have gotten you involved in this mess."

Heat flared beneath his ribs. Now, that was total nonsense. "Well, you can drop that idea right now. I'm in law enforcement, so it's my job to get involved in other people's messes." The idea of her trying to handle this on her own—

"I'm going back to Chicago." She sat up straighter and wiped a hand across her cheeks. "As soon as I get a ride back to Interior, I'll pack up and head home. Deal with the problem there."

And get killed within hours.

He took a slow breath. Reacting in anger or panic wouldn't help convince her what a terrible idea this was. "We agreed I would come with you to look for the evidence together."

She shook her head. "I can't keep putting you in danger. I can't be the cause of something happening to you. What if you had..." She bit her upper lip as more tears pooled in her eyes. "What if you had died?"

He reached for her again, and this time she took his hand. He curled his fingers around hers, so small and cold. "It's okay. I didn't die. And you don't have to face this alone."

She wouldn't meet his gaze.

He squeezed her hand. "God is with us. He sent help at just the right time earlier today. And if the worst happens to me, I'd gladly make that sacrifice doing what's right. That's part of being in law enforcement—giving up my own rights to help others. There's always a risk, but we take it because we want to defend the innocent and catch the bad guys. It's who I am."

"You are a remarkable man, Micah Ellis." She pulled her hand away, brushed her cheeks, and lifted her green gaze to his. Something flickered in her eyes, something that caught him completely off guard—a depth of feeling that simultaneously terrified and thrilled him. Warmth surged along the back of his neck, and he found it hard to meet her gaze.

Surely it was all in his head, though. They'd been through a lot. It only stood to reason they'd be swept up in the moment. Once things settled down and he felt more levelheaded, he'd realize she only meant to compliment him. Thank him.

But the only thing that mattered right now was keeping Abigail safe. If he kept the focus on helping her and Owen, she'd be able to move on with her life. And he wouldn't relive the past.

He looked back at her. "So, you're not going to Chicago alone, got it? You're going to wait until they let me out of here, and then we're going together. Besides, if it makes you feel any better, after what they did to my Visitor Center, this case is my jurisdiction now."

She nodded slowly, eyes shining.

"Promise?" he asked.

"I promise."

The sky was still dark by the time the doctor released him, but the faintest milky blue in the east hinted at the day to come. Micah and Abigail went over the details of the previous night's attack with the sheriff's department, although Abigail had already given them the basics while they'd waited for the ambulance.

Chief Ranger Langston offered to pick them up at the hospital and drive them back to Interior, which meant retelling everything again without sleep but saved them a meeting in the morning. At least Micah could get out complete sentences now without hacking. His throat and sinuses still felt itchy and abused, but the extra oxygen had helped his lungs. Thankfully, Abigail hadn't inhaled as much smoke, so she hadn't needed oxygen.

By noon, they'd managed to throw a couple of overnight bags into Micah's car and start on the long drive to Chicago.

"Sorry it's such a mess in here," he apologized for the fifteenth time. "I'm not used to having passengers."

Abigail had found yet another granola bar wrapper—they seemed to be leaking out of the seat cushion seams—and stuffed it into a cup holder in the center console. "It's okay. I appreciate you offering to take your car."

Unfortunately it made the most sense, with how recognizable Abigail's car would be to any pursuers. So they'd have to suffer through the thirteen-hour drive in his beat-up old Honda Accord, with the scattered trash he hadn't had time to fully remove and the air conditioning that only worked when it was in the mood.

"I'm not usually this messy," he said, by way of another apology. The car had been due for a good cleaning for a while, he just hadn't gotten to it. Why did he feel obliged to make sure she knew that? "And I normally use a park service vehicle for work."

She smiled, a ray of sunshine after a long night. "I know. I saw the inside of your house, remember? I really liked your coffee table, by the way."

"Thanks. Another woodworking project with my dad. We used a slab from a big old oak tree that had stood in our yard for ages before a storm took it down. He's got a matching one."

"You made it? That's really impressive." Something about her tone made his mind leap to her husband. Had Eric been the same? Someone who loved working with his hands? It wasn't a comparison he wanted to make.

"Working with my hands gives my mind a break. It almost becomes time for meditation and prayer, if that makes sense. Like I can forget about all of life's drama and focus on the Lord while my hands are busy."

And he'd had a lot to forget. He glanced at Abigail to find her watching him, a speculative gleam in her eyes. Like she wanted to know about his past but was too polite to ask.

He shifted in his seat and cleared his throat. Better to change the topic right now.

But the next words that popped out of his mouth weren't what his brain had intended. "I, uh, told you I worked in Utah before this? At Arches National Park?"

She nodded, sitting up a little straighter.

"There was a woman at my church who played in the worship band. Younger than me. Really passionate about life and the Lord. Adventurous. Cute." He glanced at Abigail, who watched him with rapt attention. She had to be wondering why he was telling her all this. Exactly what *he* was wondering. But the words kept spewing out, almost on their own. "We started dating. Found out we had all these things in common. We'd go mountain biking, hiking, skiing. Anyway, things got serious fast. We were spending all this time together, doing stuff. Sometimes she'd have other plans and she wouldn't elaborate, but I didn't think anything of it. Figured she was with her friends."

Abigail's throat bobbed, and the expression in her eyes shifted. Like she guessed where this story was heading.

He pressed on. "So, I bought a ring. Spent nearly all my savings. My term at Arches was almost up, and I thought for sure she was God's provision for my life. But when I proposed…" He clenched his teeth, then let out a short sigh. "She said she was dating another man at the same time, someone she'd met online. That she'd thought we were just having fun."

"Oh, Micah." Abigail's fingers pressed to her mouth, and pain radiated from her gaze. "What did you do?"

"Pawned the ring. First and only time I've ever set foot in one of those places. Then I got stationed here. Last time I saw her was my final morning at church when she was leading worship up front. I wished her the best and moved on."

Or moved away. Because he hadn't truly moved on, had he? His heart was still tied up in that moment when she'd rejected him, and hot shame had coated every inch of his insides like sticky tar. *Help me to forgive her, Lord.*

"I'm so sorry." Abigail's soft words cut into his thoughts. "I don't know what she was thinking. She obviously didn't see how amazing you are, or she never would've let you go."

"Thanks." Warmth burned the back of his neck at her words. She had to say that to be polite, but that didn't stop her words from soothing some of the ache inside. In fact, just sharing about Taylor made him feel better. He had friends who knew the gist of the story, but not the full extent of what it had cost him.

"And I know this might not feel like much consolation, but it's better you found out how she felt before she married you." She pressed her lips together. "Once you take those vows before God…" Her voice trailed off, and she gazed out the window.

"Was that what happened?" The question burst out before he considered whether she'd want to talk about it. "Between you and Eric?"

She pressed her lips together and nodded. "He was so romantic when we were dating, sending me flowers, making reservations at fancy restaurants, taking me for walks in the park. When he proposed, I thought he was offering everything I'd wanted. But…" She inhaled sharply, then let out a slow breath. "It didn't take long to realize the real Eric was a different person, and that I didn't know him at all. Who knows, maybe he thought the same thing about me."

Silence settled over them as he scrambled for something to say, something to help ease the pain she'd lived with for so many years. But a bandage of words wouldn't fix a gaping wound.

Before he could come up with anything, she cleared her throat, then reached for her purse near her feet. "Anyway, while we were at the hospital, I did some thinking about those files."

Good, he wasn't the only one ready to retreat to safety. Why had he spilled that whole story about Taylor? Or pried into her marriage? This was hardly a sound plan for keeping her at arm's length.

"Great," he said, a little too enthusiastically. "What have you got?"

After rummaging in her purse for a moment, she pulled out a folded piece of paper. "Remember those references to Key West? Maybe instead of referring to location, he meant it as a clue to find the key. There's a conch shell we bought on that trip, upstairs on the bathroom counter. It's big enough it could easily hide a key. It never occurred to me before."

The tone of her voice remained steady, conversational almost—like she wasn't drowning in memories over the loss of her husband, but there had to be so much there still to unpack. That wasn't his place, though. Not now...not ever.

"Good idea," he said, keeping his tone casual. "Sounds plausible to me."

She smiled, but an awkward silence settled between them. Unasked questions and unspoken thoughts swirled. Worst of all was this insistent urge to take her small hand from where it rested on her leg and wrap it in his own.

He tapped a button on his steering wheel to increase the car's cruise control speed. The sooner they got to Chicago, the sooner they could find Eric's files and free Abigail from the threat hovering over her.

She'd be able to get Owen back and return to her life, and he'd be able to do the same. Back to the safety of singleness, behind the walls he'd worked so hard to construct.

It was the best possible ending for them, the thing he wanted most.

And he'd keep telling himself that every single day until she was home.

SEVEN

The bungalow looked exactly the way Abigail remembered, every Craftsman-style detail etched into her brain, every contour and line bearing the trace of Eric's influence on her adult life. For the last week, she'd imagined coming back here, how good it would feel to be somewhere familiar—to be home—but now there was only a stale smell in the air and a knot in her stomach. A raw, gnawing ache that insistently reminded her of how much she'd struggled here. How hard she'd tried to make him happy, to create a life for herself and Owen despite the pain of her marriage, all while slowly losing herself.

She hadn't even realized it had happened, but now, standing in her entryway with Eric gone and life upside-down, she could see clearly how her entire life here had been overshadowed by him. By the stress of his changing moods, by his hopes and wants, by her attempts to keep him happy and engaged with her and Owen. Somewhere in the middle of it all, she'd lost sight of the things *she* wanted in life. Probably because Eric had never asked. Even when they'd been dating, his focus had been mainly on himself—showing her how charming and romantic he could be, rather than truly getting to know each other. And she'd fallen right for it.

"Are you okay?" Micah's gentle tone cut into her thoughts. For a second she had to resist the impulse to step closer to him. The last thing she needed was to trade away this newfound freedom before she'd even had a chance to evaluate it. Yes, it was terrifying— but it was also an opportunity to reshape her life into what she wanted it to be. Almost like, in the midst of all this awfulness, God was offering her a gift. A second chance.

The thought caught her off guard. *Was* God working behind the scenes? This whole time, when she'd thought He was ignoring her, had He been there all along? It was too much to assess right now, with Micah watching her.

"I… Yeah, sorry." She glanced at him but just as quickly looked away. The tender concern in his blue eyes was *not* helping her resolve. Had Eric ever looked at her that way?

"There are a lot of memories here. I guess I wasn't quite prepared."

"You have every reason to feel that way. Besides, it's been a long day. Night. Whatever."

Three in the morning, according to the big grandfather clock standing against the staircase leading to the second floor. They'd driven straight through from Interior, only stopping for gas and to grab a quick bite to eat.

She nodded, then turned to Micah. "If you want to come in and get settled in the living room, I'll run upstairs and check the conch shell."

"It's okay if you want to wait till morning," he offered. "We had a long drive. The bank won't open until then anyway."

"I need to know if it's there. Otherwise, I have to figure out where else to look." Which sounded utterly hopeless—after all, she'd already searched through all of Eric's things for the files, so wouldn't she have noticed a random key? Too bad he didn't carry it on his key ring, which was the first place she'd checked.

Flipping on the lights, she led the way into their living room. The stone fireplace and exposed ceiling beams had been her idea when they bought the house so many years ago, and the space still evoked the same sense of welcoming coziness she'd always loved. It had become her refuge on the lonely winter nights when Eric worked late. She scooped up some blankets out of a big basket near the hearth and carried them to the leather sectional. "There's a bathroom back there on the right, next to the office. Do you need anything else?"

His gaze met hers, and her breath stalled. Even after fifteen hours in the car and a near-death by fire the previous night, the man was still as attractive on the outside as he was on the inside. Why had that woman in Utah ever let him go?

Thankfully he didn't appear to notice her useless thoughts. "No," he said. "I'm good. Do you want me to come up with you? To make sure the second floor is clear? Or I can wait down here. It's up to you."

She glanced back at the entryway, with its beveled glass chandelier hanging over the staircase leading up to the dark second floor. The exterior of the house had looked fine when they arrived, with no sign of another break-in. Micah had parked on the street a few houses down so it wouldn't be as obvious she'd returned. Still, the thought of trudging up there in the darkness alone, with all those memories...

She tipped her head. "If you don't mind. Thank you."

He dropped his bag next to the couch and followed her to the entryway, then up the hardwood staircase to the second level. The wood still gleamed, despite a week's absence, but they had to dodge toy cars and stuffed animals once they reached the landing. Seeing Owen's things made her heart ache. He was the innocent victim in all of this.

"Sorry about the mess," she said softly.

Instead of answering, Micah caught her hand in his, gave it a squeeze, and released. His silent way of saying it was okay?

Checking the upstairs didn't take long—there were only two bedrooms and two bathrooms, along with the sitting-slash-play area on the landing. She went to Owen's room first, her knees nearly buckling at the sight of all his familiar things. The smell was wrong, though—all stuffy and musty and hot after being shut up for a week.

Her and Eric's room looked the way it always did—bed neatly made up with its white matelassé coverlet, side tables impeccably clean. Her heart curled again, but this time it wasn't the same ache of longing as she felt for

Owen. Instead, it was regret, and this surging sense of freedom tinged with guilt. Shouldn't she feel more sorrow?

"In here." She led the way to the big bathroom with its two-sink vanity counter. The pink-and-cream conch shell sat in the center beneath the mirror. Sparks shot through her nerves as she picked it up. If they could just find that key...

She slipped her fingers inside, feeling along the smooth interior of the shell. She repeated the action a second time.

Nothing.

With a sigh, she shook her head and set it back on the counter. How could Eric *do* this to her? To Owen? Pent-up frustration rattled through her insides, swelling like a balloon about to burst. She pressed her fingers to her mouth. "It's not there. And I have no idea where else to look."

Micah ran a hand through his hair. "It's okay. We'll find it. We'll get started first thing tomorrow and—"

"*Where?*" The word exploded out, catching even her off guard. Anger had never been her go-to response—usually she felt shame, absorbing and internalizing the other person's feelings—but not anymore. She'd had enough.

She shoved past Micah and beelined for the stairs. A part of her knew she wasn't acting much older than Owen in the midst of one of his tantrums, but she couldn't help it. Not after everything Eric had done.

"What was he *thinking*? Why didn't he run for the cops the second he realized who David wanted him to work for?" She savored the loud thump of each footstep down the wooden staircase. Micah followed silently behind. "And why on earth would he think I'd know where to find this stupid key and safe deposit box?"

She led the way into the living room, but there was no way she could sit. Not now. She rounded on Micah, as if he somehow had the answers.

He leaned against the oak trim of the doorway and watched her, his blue eyes thoughtful. "Maybe he didn't know who they were at first. And by the time he did, he was in too deep. And the key... He couldn't risk letting them find it."

It was a perfectly rational explanation, one she'd considered herself, but the angry monster in her chest didn't care. Because that wasn't the real heart of the betrayal, was it? Flames scorched up her esophagus, burning her sinuses until tears pooled in her eyes. "Why didn't he love me?"

The words wrenched themselves out of her soul like a rotten tooth being pulled. Her vision grew blurry and liquid coursed down her cheeks, salty and hot against her lips. What had she done wrong to push him away?

How had she failed so badly?

"Is that why God doesn't love me either?" she choked out through tears.

Strong arms wrapped around her, filling her senses with the subtle scents of cypress and cool peppermint. She pressed her cheek against the soft cotton of his shirt and squeezed her eyes shut as her shoulders shook. If only she could stay like this, warm and safe in his embrace, but no amount of crying or accepting comfort was going to change the facts. Or help Owen.

So she lifted her head and shifted her hands to press against his chest. He loosened his grip, allowing her to pull away, but his hands lingered on her arms as his gaze drilled into hers with an intensity that stilled her breath.

"Abigail Fox, this is not your fault. I don't know what happened between you and Eric, but he was a fool not to fight for you. Not to give everything he had for you. You are…" He shook his head, then glanced up at the ceiling as if collecting his thoughts. "An amazing mother and woman. Strong. Gentle. Intelligent. Thoughtful. Gorgeous. And I—"

His eyes found hers again and suddenly she was swimming in a sea of blue that threatened to sweep her away. A swarm of butterflies let loose in her stomach when his gaze dropped to her mouth. With each tender word he'd just said, she'd drifted closer to him, until their faces were only inches apart.

When he dipped his chin lower, it was only natural to lift her mouth to meet his. Their lips brushed, the merest whisper of a kiss, but the room sparked with electricity. Heady delight filled her senses, leaving her wanting more. Until—

What on earth was she *doing*? She sprang back and he let his hands fall, his eyes wide to the point of panic. Her fingers drifted to her still-tingling lips as a barrage of barely coherent thoughts flooded her brain.

Micah pressed his hands to the top of his head, still backing away from her, as if there were no physical way to put enough space between them.

She glanced around the room, anywhere but at him, and her gaze landed on a picture of Owen on the fireplace mantel. What would he think, if he knew what his mom was doing when she was supposed to be finding those files and getting him back?

And Eric? She hadn't kissed another man in *years*. Shouldn't she feel a greater sense of loss? Guilt riddled her insides.

Behind her, Micah cleared his throat. "I'm sorry all this has happened to you and Owen. You didn't deserve it." He walked over to the sectional and picked up his bag, his motions stiff and mechanical.

What on earth had just happened?

They were here to find those files, and then they'd be saying goodbye. There was no alternative ending to this story.

Damage control. That was all Micah could think about as he tugged a hoodie out of his bag and slipped it over his head. Like an extra layer of defense between him and this distraught woman whom he wanted nothing more than to comfort and hold close. And keep kissing, if he was being brutally honest.

But the way she'd looked at him as she backed away, like he was a rattlesnake ready to strike… Emotions tumbled through his chest, too fast to process.

He knew opening up to her about Taylor earlier had been a dangerous idea, but he'd had no clue the ice was *this* thin. Any second now they'd tumble through into freezing cold waters and end up risking everything. Or she'd reject him completely, pushing him out of her life to the point where he couldn't even help her and Owen.

The important thing now was to backpedal, distance himself but still help her.

Because he *had* to help her. She needed safety, of course, but also to know that not everyone was like her late husband. Not everyone cared more about themselves than the important people in their life. Or failed to even recognize those people as important.

And most definitely, with 100 percent certainty, God loved her. *Please help her to see that, Lord.* No amount of him telling her that would help her internalize it, though. That was God's work.

He plumped a couple of pillows on the end of the leather sofa before turning back to face her. She was staring at a point on the stone fireplace as if lost in thought.

When she spoke again, she didn't look at him. Just kept staring at the stonework. "The worst part is, things had gotten so bad by the end, it's almost a relief that he's gone. That's terrible to say, isn't it? But it's the truth. I could never make him happy."

"It wasn't your job to make him happy. Relationships are about sacrificing for the other person because you love them, not demanding that they meet your needs." At least, that was the way God intended things, according to His Word. Whether that ever played out in real life… Well, he hadn't seen much of it.

"We started out well. I thought he was the right one for me…" Her gaze collided with his, and her eyes were twin pools of liquid green. "Is that what happens to every relationship?"

Wrong person to ask. He rubbed the back of his neck and sat heavily on the couch. "I…" He paused, stalling for time as he scrambled to come up with something hopeful and uplifting, but why lie to her? God never promised happiness in this life, did He? Rather, the joy and hope of His presence. There were no guarantees when it came to human love, as he'd seen again and again. "To be honest, you probably shouldn't ask me, because in my experience, yeah. It is. You know what happened between me and Taylor. My parents didn't fare any better."

An alarm in the back of his mind told him to shut his mouth, but he kept going. Why not let it all out now? He'd already blown it with that kiss. "When my mom left us, I kept expecting her to come back. I remember this one year, I think I was twelve or thirteen, and I was convinced she'd show up for my birthday. No matter what Dad said, I didn't believe him. Mom was coming back. Finally, my dad pulled me aside from my friends." The memory was so vivid he could still feel the exact moment all hope had shattered. "He told me she was gone. Murdered. She'd moved in with some guy in Fort Collins and he'd beaten her to death six months after she left us. The guy had already been in jail three years. And I never knew. Here I'd been blaming my dad for keeping her away all that time." A muscle twitched in his jaw. "That's how relationships end."

He stared down at his hands, refusing to meet her gaze, but finally the silence broke him. When he looked up, she was biting her lip, nostrils flaring. Red hot shame pierced his ribs, and along with it, the almost unbearable urge to pull her into his arms and never let her go.

Which would be the antithesis of everything he'd just communicated.

So he dug into his bag, pulled out a toothbrush, and said, "We should try to get some sleep."

She nodded, her throat bobbing. "I'll be upstairs." Her footsteps padded softly across the floor and up the stairs.

Micah lay awake for a long time, staring at the ceiling, until he finally drifted into a restless sleep.

Despite the late night, he woke early the next morning from light streaming in around the edges of the wooden blinds. The rest of the house was silent, so he headed for the kitchen and rummaged through the cabinets until he found whole coffee beans and a grinder. Coffee was a must running on only a few hours' sleep. As the scent filled the kitchen, he breathed deeply, offering up another prayer for Abigail.

This morning, though, the words felt like they didn't make it past the ceiling. Like there was some obstacle blocking his sense of intimacy with his Creator. *What's up, Lord?* With a fresh sense of uncertainty, he replayed last night's conversation with Abigail in his mind. That moment where he'd sealed off his heart again, told her relationships were doomed to fail…

But what was wrong with being honest? They *were* doomed to fail, and he didn't want any part of that kind of heartbreak again. Sure, she wasn't anything like Taylor, or his mom, but that didn't mean something else couldn't go wrong.

Wasn't it natural to protect yourself?

Before he could sort it out, soft footsteps padded down the stairs. A moment later Abigail appeared, no less beautiful for the dark smudges under her eyes or her tousled hair. She was already dressed in a pair of wide-leg striped pants and a coordinating navy blue shirt that highlighted her lovely facial features.

She smiled, then nodded toward the coffee maker. "Let me grab some mugs."

Some floral scent followed her as she passed him and opened one of the cabinets, and he inhaled deeply before catching himself. Had he not listened to anything he'd told himself last night?

Hopefully the coffee would clear his head. He backed up a few paces to give her space as she poured two steaming mugs and handed one to him. The strong, nutty aroma wafted through the air and he breathed it in, trying to reset his uncooperative brain.

"Any new ideas come to you?" he asked.

She took a slow sip, then tipped her head toward the living room. "I want to check a photo album." The words came out matter-of-fact—like she too wanted to forget the emotional carnage of the previous night. "That Key West trip was a long time ago. Our honeymoon." Her cheeks turned faint red. "Back before Eric finished his MBA and got the job in Chicago. Anyway, maybe if I look at the pictures, it will jog my memory."

Fifteen minutes later, after digging up some granola bars in the pantry for breakfast, they sat down at the dining room table with a photo book. The spine read "Our Honeymoon" in a loopy, cursive font. On the cover, a man with light brown hair had his arm wrapped around a younger Abigail's shoulders. Her smile was so huge it was almost giddy—so different from the worried expression the current circumstances forced her to wear.

It was hard to watch as she flipped the pages. Hard to see how happy she had been, knowing how the story ended. And if he was being honest, it was hard to witness the past she'd experienced with this other man who hadn't loved her the way she deserved. He caught himself cracking his knuckles under the table and forced his hands apart.

And what about Abigail? This had to be even harder for *her*. He stole a glance at her, but her face was a mask of concentration. Almost like she'd been able to compartmentalize her emotions and—

"That's it." She clapped her hands together.

"What?"

She pointed to a picture in the album. Eric, up on a tiny stage, holding a microphone with a funny, crooning look on his face. "That night. We had conch sandwiches at this hole-in-the-wall restaurant, and they had karaoke. I dared Eric to sing. When he was done, he gave me a locket. I don't know why I didn't think of it before."

"Do you have the locket?" Her skin was bare around her collarbone, and he'd never noticed her wearing a necklace.

"Upstairs, in my dresser. I stopped wearing it when Owen was born because he was always tugging on the chain." She pushed away from the table, and he followed as she jogged up the stairs to the master bedroom.

After rummaging in one of the dresser drawers for a minute, she pulled out a black velvet case. The color shifted in her cheeks as she opened it, revealing a small gold heart locket attached to a chain.

He frowned. "A key wouldn't fit in that."

"No, but it would fit underneath." She lifted the velvet-covered cardboard to expose the chain beneath—

And a small brass key.

She gasped softly. "But what bank is it at?"

"Is there a note with the address? Maybe inside the locket?"

With a small click, she popped the heart open. A piece of paper fluttered out and they both reached for it, their fingers brushing together. Micah pulled back, letting her pick it up. She set the locket and case down on the dresser top and unfolded the paper, holding it out so they could both read it.

PNC Bank, 100 W Randolph.

Forgive me.

Her throat bobbed and she blinked rapidly, then balled the key and note up in her hand. "Let's go."

They took the L train to reach the bank, which was located downtown, not far from Eric's office. Abigail clutched her handbag close to her side as she held on to a bar near the train's door. The train slowed, and as soon as the doors opened, she hopped out onto the platform, Micah right behind her.

He kept close as she wove through the crowds, up the stairs, and into the bright morning sunlight. Even though the feeling didn't articulate itself into the words of a prayer, an impression of gratitude lingered in her heart.

God could have left her to do all this alone, but He hadn't. Maybe He *hadn't* completely abandoned her. He'd sent someone to help.

Someone with muscles and a gun and law enforcement training. Someone who was warm-hearted, funny, kind, and generous. And attractive to the point of trouble.

But she needed to peel her thoughts away from Micah's good qualities and instead focus on checking over her shoulder to keep watch as they navigated the busy sidewalk. Didn't seem to matter what time of day it was when you were on a Chicago street, it would be crowded. And who knew how many of these random passersby worked for the mafia?

The thought chilled some of the warmth stirring in her chest. She breathed easier once they reached the bank, went through the revolving door, and stepped into the cool interior. Two armed security guards on either side of the lobby added to her sense of reassurance.

Check the box, recover the evidence, and get out of the city.

Easy-peasy.

Her nerves felt strung out like a taut wire as they followed a clerk to the vaults and the safe deposit box in the back of the bank. With her name listed as trustee, all she'd had to do was prove her identity and produce the key to gain access.

Such a simple thing after all these weeks of confusion and running.

Her gaze met Micah's as they waited at a table in the vault while the employee brought out the box. He set it down on the table with a clang, then stepped back to give her space to inspect the contents.

Her fingers trembled as she lifted the metal lid.

Inside were two envelopes—a large manila one and a smaller letter-size one. She collapsed back into her seat and pressed a hand to her heart. This hadn't all been for nothing. A smile tugged at Micah's lips.

She removed the envelopes, setting the smaller one aside and opening the large one first. As she pulled out the contents—a stack of file folders—a flash drive slid out onto the table. Her heart skipped. Surely this was what they needed. She set the files on the table between her and Micah, then opened them one at a time.

Spreadsheets. Photocopies of receipts. Tax forms. Emails and logs of phone conversations. As meticulous as Eric had been in nearly every area of life.

"This is it." She glanced at Micah, raising her eyebrows. "Exactly what we need."

He held up the flash drive. "Along with the digital backup."

"Take a look at this…" She slid one of the

sheets across the table to him. The header at the top read, "Known or Suspected to Be in the Outfit's Pay."

His eyes went wide and he let out a low whistle as his finger traced the list of names, stopping at—

James Bernetto. The Chicago cop who'd handled Eric's death.

Anger burned in her gut. That man *was* working for the mob. Maybe one of these many other records could prove it.

Micah's lips formed a thin, white line as he handed her back the sheet. She slid the stack of files inside the envelope and secured it with the metal clasp.

"We'll make sure these get into the right hands," he said grimly. Then his gaze fell on the other envelope. "What's in there? Unless you'd rather read it in private." He started to back his chair away, but she stopped him, placing a hand on his arm.

"No, it's okay. I don't mind if you see." The reality hit her like a ton of bricks—if there was any person she wanted at her side right now, it was him. Not even her sister or her friends from church would understand the way Micah would. He'd been through almost all of this with her, the worst time in her life. A steady rock of support.

She braced herself as she opened the envelope. Would it be another apology? A confession? Eric had already asked for her forgiveness, and she would give it, in time. Maybe one day she'd even start to understand what had happened in his life.

The folded sheaf of papers inside was several pages thick, and this time, to her relief, there was no handwritten note. Only a formal cover letter listing the contents of the envelope, from an attorney she'd never heard of in Switzerland. It took her a moment to fully register what the typed letters said.

She looked up at Micah, her forehead crinkling. His eyes went wide as he glanced between her and the contents.

Eric had an offshore bank account worth nearly seven figures, and *she* was the named trustee.

Her throat went dry. "That's where the money they paid him went. It certainly never hit our shared accounts." She balled a hand into a fist. "How much trouble will this get me into with the IRS?"

Instead of answering, Micah took the stack of papers and flipped through it. "I'm not sure it will. Look—he filed FATCA forms. He declared the account. My guess is, he was trying to protect it from the mob, not the government."

"But how did he claim the income when it was paid by the mafia?" For once, she wished she'd paid attention to their taxes. But Eric had been an accountant—it had never occurred to her to question him.

He scratched his chin through the thick bristles of his beard. "We'll have to access the individual 1040s to figure that out. Maybe he listed it as a consulting fee. Or several. Spread out over a number of years, it might not have been red flagged." He leaned back in his chair. "Absolutely we should report this to the FBI along with these—" he tapped the stack of files "—but I'd be surprised if they have a case to seize the funds. Especially with your innocence."

As much as she hated where that money had come from, there was no denying how much she and Owen needed it. Especially since the life insurance claim had been denied after the police ruled Eric's death a suicide. But there was no point in daydreaming right now—not with Owen far away and their lives on the line. Finances could wait.

She pulled out the prepaid phone and snapped a picture of the bank account information and attorney's name, just in case something happened to the papers. Then she refolded the stack and placed it back in the envelope. "Now what? How do we get these somewhere safe?"

"As soon as we leave the vault and get back to cell service, I'll let Brian know we found your husband's files. He'll set up the meeting with an FBI agent in Rapid City. All we need to do is get back to my car and head home." He cleared his throat. "I mean, back to Interior."

She smiled, trying to alleviate his discomfort. Truth was, Interior almost felt as much like home as Chicago did now. Sure, her house and all her things were here, but everything bore stamps of the past, the imprint of her time with Eric. Good *had* come out of it—Owen was living proof—but she was ready to leave. Ready to move on and make a new life for herself, apart from Eric and his bad decisions. Instead of terrifying her, as it had a few weeks ago, the thought of starting fresh, finding a home, getting back into teaching… It sent a thrill of excitement zipping through her system. Maybe God *could* work all things out for the good, even the darkest situations.

The sun was high overhead by the time they exited the bank, one of those muggy

Chicago summer days where the pavement felt like it could singe your feet through your shoes. She'd stowed the files and flash drive in her handbag, and now clutched it close to her body as they navigated the crowded streets back to the L.

She kept watch as Micah paid for their train tickets, but there was no sign of pursuers. Was it possible they'd actually slipped into the city and recovered the evidence undetected? But she couldn't breathe easy yet, not until they were back on the road to South Dakota and away from this hive of mob activity.

Micah's cell phone chimed as they boarded the train. "Good, Brian got my text. He's setting up the meeting."

She slid into an empty seat and glanced over her shoulder as he sat next to her.

Wait. That man behind them at the back of the train car—he was watching them. She stiffened, a chill sweeping across her arms as the train dropped down into the darkness of a tunnel. Artificial orange light from the train's ceiling reflected off the plastic seats.

His dark eyes locked onto her face, over the top of a magazine. Watching.

Had they been found?

EIGHT

Micah settled into the hard seat, grateful they'd found the files. And with Eric's money stashed away in the bank—if Abigail got to keep it—she and Owen would be set for a long time.

He flinched as she laid her head on his shoulder, the movement catching him by surprise. Must be the stress of the day getting to her. His beard brushed against her silky hair as he glanced down at her.

"You okay?"

"Back of the train," she whispered. "The man with the magazine. He's watching us."

Every nerve went taut as he pressed a kiss to the top of Abigail's head, a pretense to allow him to see the man out of the corner of his eye. The man shifted the magazine, like he was flipping pages, but his gaze barely glanced down before refocusing on Micah and Abigail.

"Do you think he recognizes us?" she asked.

He lifted his head, shaking off the scent of her floral shampoo like cobwebs clouding his brain. "Maybe. But I don't think he'll make a move with other people on the train. Keep your head on my shoulder so he can't see your face."

"We can try to lose him when we transfer to the red line. Either at the next stop or Belmont." She flicked her finger toward a big map of the train system on the other side of the door.

"What are we on now?"

"Purple. It's an express, so it goes past our stop. See how purple, red, and brown run parallel heading north? We could even hop onto brown if we need to."

He sucked on his lower lip. "What about getting back to the car?" The last thing they wanted to do was give up precious time racing through the city. But staying here, where the mobster could keep an eye on them and notify his pals, wasn't at the top of Micah's list either.

"We can transfer back to red at Belmont," Abigail said. "Or leave the station and take a cab."

The train was slowing, approaching the station. They had to decide fast. He lowered his head to kiss her hair again, ignoring the way his heart turned over at the contact, and instead glanced at the man. He was still watching, but this time his gaze darted from them toward the front of the car.

Where a second man was visible through the glass doors, working his way toward their car.

Micah pressed his cheek to Abigail's head. "Don't panic, but another one's coming. Next car up. He's almost to the doors."

"We've got to run," she whispered.

"Stay seated until the doors open, then we go at the last second. Maximize our chances."

She nodded. Kept her head on his shoulder, but now he could feel the tension flowing off her in waves as the train crawled toward the platform. He wrapped his hand around hers and she squeezed it tightly.

The train stopped and the doors opened. Every one of his muscles tensed. "Now."

He launched out of his seat and darted for the doors, Abigail keeping pace beside him. Then onto the platform in the blazing summer sun. The man from the back of the train car had abandoned any pretense of reading and was bolting for the doors, while the other man had managed to enter their compartment.

Micah tugged Abigail's hand and pulled her away from the train. The doors were closing—*thank You, Lord*—but at the last second one of the men squeezed through and leaped onto the platform.

"One of them made it off the train," he called. "Which way?"

"Here." She pulled him toward a set of stairs in the center of the platform. "Two minutes until a red train arrives."

They raced down, dodging mothers with little kids and people dressed in suits on their way to business lunches. Behind them, someone shouted. They rushed across the tiled floor to another set of stairs leading up, praying the train would arrive before their pursuer.

Micah ushered Abigail in front of him as they swung around the railing and onto the staircase. Feet pounded across the tiles—their pursuer was coming, hard on their trail. *Please send the train, Lord*, he prayed as they burst out onto the raised platform. A handful of people were waiting, but no telltale rumble indicated the train's arrival.

"Is it late?" he asked her, alarm spiking through his system. There was nowhere to hide on the platform.

She massaged a stitch in her side, gasping for breath. Then shook her head and pointed at train headlights in the distance, moving from the direction they'd just come. "I'm sorry, wrong platform. It's on that side." A question crinkled across her forehead. "What do we do?"

Pounding on the stairs. Their pursuer was coming.

Micah watched the approaching train, gauging its speed, then grabbed Abigail's hand. "Jump the tracks. There's a ladder on the other side. Look."

Her eyes widened but she didn't argue. Instead, she tugged him forward and ran right up to the edge then dropped down and lowered herself over the side. He followed, jumping the five feet down onto the tracks.

"Don't touch the third rail!" She pointed at the interior metal strip that carried all the voltage.

"Got it," Micah said. "Now go!"

They raced across the first set, hopping over all the rails just to be safe.

"Hey, stop!" a passenger called from up on the platform. "You shouldn't—"

"Out of the way!" Their pursuer appeared above, elbowing his way through the bystanders.

The train was approaching, a massive metal beast heading straight for them.

"Hurry!" Micah called. "This way!" He gestured wildly at the maintenance ladder and guided Abigail ahead, nearly stumbling over the last non-electrified track. Behind them, the man dropped down from the platform with a *thud*. The approaching train's brakes screeched, its headlights glowing like twin suns. Way too close.

They scrambled up the metal rungs of the ladder and onto the platform with seconds to spare. Abigail bent over, hands braced on her knees and breathing hard. Through the blurred windows of the stopping train, their pursuer was visible standing on the opposite track, a cell phone pressed to his ear.

Micah's stomach dropped even as the train's doors popped open in front of them. They weren't done yet. He pointed to the man as they boarded. "We're going to have company soon."

Abigail studied the system map on the interior wall. "We're still heading north. If we can make it a few more stops without them boarding, we'll be to our station."

The train was already slowing for the next station. *Lord, please don't let them get to the train in time.*

"Do you see anyone?" she asked as people streamed on and off the train cars.

"Not yet." But every one of his muscles stayed taut as he surveyed the crowd on the platform. The doors closed and the train moved on. As another station came and went, he relaxed a little. Maybe their pursuers hadn't been able to cut them off.

"Do you think we lost them?" Abigail asked.

"I hope so." Then a new thought occurred to him. "We'd better not go back to your house, though. They're most likely watching it." Or worse, waiting inside. Thankfully he'd had the foresight to park a block away. "Is there anything in there you need?"

She stared at the back of the seat in front of them for a second, then shook her head. "I can live without that stuff."

They both stiffened at each stop, as the doors opened and passengers stepped on and off the train, but there was no one who appeared suspicious. Still, he wouldn't be able to fully relax until they were back on the interstate leaving Illinois. Check that—he wouldn't relax until the men after Abigail were safely behind bars.

If they could just get this information out of the city and into the FBI's hands, Abigail could begin the process of rebuilding her life.

Without him. The thought hurt, not a sharp

and sudden pang, but a steady gnawing ache that wouldn't go away. But it was better to be safe than have your heart utterly decimated. Wasn't it?

Abigail perched on the edge of the hard seat, counting the stops until they could exit. Despite the success of the morning, nothing felt right between her and Micah. She should *not* have kissed him. Every conversation, every look and smile, only reinforced that they were skimming over the surface of a lake full of unspoken things. Better this way, though, wasn't it? Lakes were dark and deep and cold, and it was safer up here in the sun.

Life lesson, compliments of one doomed marriage. No reason to go after another one that could fail. And now that they had the files, they only had to work together a little while longer.

She glanced again at the map, then at the approaching train station. "This is our stop. Once we exit the station, we can catch a bus to reach my street."

The train slowed, and they stood then exited. This platform was busier than the last few, but all they had to do was get down the stairs, reach the buses, and soon they'd be back to Micah's car. Maybe they'd actually make it.

The train pulled away and she headed for the door that would lead them down into the station. She turned back to look for Micah, but he'd gotten separated by a group of college students.

Someone bumped into her from behind, and she stumbled across the scuffed linoleum. As she struggled to regain her balance, she crashed into a dark-haired man lurking near the corner.

Wait—she recognized him. The man who'd been on the train earlier "reading" the magazine. He'd caught up with them. Her heart skyrocketed into her throat as she tried to push away from him, but a press of people threading through the narrow passageway kept her from moving.

He smirked. "We're taking a walk."

"I'm not going anywhere with—"

Something sharp jabbed through the soft fabric of her shirt, threatening her ribs.

"I'd shut up if I were you." Her attacker's hot breath blew against her ear, sending a shiver of revulsion down her spine. "We're heading out of here together." He spun her around toward the stairs and wrapped his arm around her back, the knife's sharp point hidden in his hand.

The door behind them opened with a whoosh of sticky summer air. "Abigail!" Micah called. *Thank You, Lord.* She glanced over her shoulder just in time to see another man coming up behind him—the same man who'd chased them through the station earlier.

"Behind you!" she yelled, but as Micah spun to face him, the man pummeled him in the stomach. She gasped as Micah doubled over.

"Security!" someone called.

Micah straightened, leveling a fist at the other man, but before she could see more, her attacker shoved her toward the stairs. The scuffling sounds behind them suddenly muted as the door to the platform slammed shut.

"Move it," the man growled, dragging her down the concrete steps. She clutched her bag tightly, her heart pounding. She couldn't let the man get her out of the station. *Or* get the files. But what to do?

The traffic on the stairs had slowed with the departure of the train, and now the staircase was empty except for the two of them.

It wouldn't be long, though, before security responded. She just had to stall until then.

As if in answer to her thoughts, the pounding of footsteps echoed from the lower level. The man pushed the tip of the knife into her back, urging her to move faster. When they reached the lower steps, the main station came into view.

Two security guards raced across the concrete floor, dodging travelers, and heading for the stairs. Abigail's mouth opened, her arm starting to raise, when the man yanked her aside and pressed the knife harder into her ribs.

"Don't say a word."

Sharp pain pierced her skin, and she bit her tongue to keep from crying out. The guards raced past, taking the steps two at a time, not even noticing the woman held hostage in plain sight.

She *had* to do something.

As the man urged her forward again, she slipped a foot sideways and let her leg tangle up with his. In an instant they both crashed onto the concrete on hands and knees, the man swearing loudly. As she fell, the handbag slipped off her shoulder and hit the ground, its contents spilling out and skittering in all directions across the smooth floor. The flash drive landed closest.

She lunged for it, but the man shoved her out of his way and swooped it up in his big hand.

"Help!" she yelled. "Police! That man is stealing from me!"

He swore again and dove for the manila envelope, but she was closer and snatched it up.

"Stop!" a voice called from the stairs as one of the security guards came running down.

The man dove for the envelope in her hand, but when his reach fell short, he glanced at the staircase and took off through the station, shoving people out of the way. Abigail clutched the envelope to her chest, hands shaking, and watched as the guard sprinted after her attacker. He'd gotten away with the flash drive, but at least the files were safe.

"Ma'am, are you all right?" An older woman touched her elbow.

She managed to nod. "Yes, thank you, I'm fine now."

A couple of bystanders helped her gather the items from her bag that had scattered across the floor. By the time the purse was safely back on her shoulder, both envelopes tucked inside, Micah came jogging down the steps. Behind him, the security guard who'd run upstairs had the other mobster in custody.

As soon as Micah's gaze fell on her, he rushed over and swept her into his arms. He held her for a long moment, her face nestled against his chest, then finally released her. His intense blue gaze scanned her face, and he opened his mouth as if to say something but then pressed his lips together.

She offered a weak smile. "I'm all right. He got away with the flash drive, but I still have the paper copies."

He touched her cheek, his fingers gently grazing her skin. "I was so worried about you. And angry at myself for letting us get separated." His jaw clenched.

The warmth of his touch helped soothe the trauma of the last ten minutes, and she leaned her face against his hand. "It's not your fault." For a split second they stood frozen that way, staring into each other's eyes, until she snapped back to her senses and pulled away. His cheek was swelling up, bruised and red on one side, and she tipped her head toward it. "We should get some ice on that."

He shrugged. "I may have taken a couple of hits."

Another security guard arrived on the scene and escorted them to a small office inside the station, where he offered Micah some ice for his cheek and took their statements. "Would you like a police escort back to your home?" he asked, reaching for the desktop phone.

She and Micah exchanged a glance, then he shook his head. "We'll be fine." Trusting the police around here was too big of a risk.

But as they caught a bus to her street, she couldn't help wondering... *Would* they be fine?

The throbbing in Micah's cheek was like a constant reminder that he'd nearly failed to protect Abigail. His heart twisted more painfully than the bruise swelling under his eye. They were so close—all he had to do was help her get those files out of the city and safely to the FBI. The end was almost in sight. But at the rate things were going, he wasn't sure they were going to make it.

They hopped off the bus a few minutes later and walked half a block to Abigail's street. The sun had peaked and was starting its westward descent, gleaming off the cars and bungalow windows on the opposite side of the street. His steps grew quicker, and lighter, as they rounded the corner and spotted his car. Just a bit more and they'd be on their way.

But they were still a few car lengths away when Abigail froze, her hand wrapping around his arm. "Micah, look. The back tire."

His heart sank. The metal rim of the wheel rested on the pavement in a puddle of slashed black rubber. And if they'd gotten one, no doubt all the tires had suffered the same fate.

He glanced quickly around the street, but there was no sign of anyone watching. Was it a random act of vandalism? Unlikely.

"Come on, quick. We'd better check the others." He took Abigail's hand and they jogged down the sidewalk, keeping close to the parked cars and scanning the houses. Sure enough, all four tires had been destroyed beyond any hope of repair. The neighboring cars were untouched.

Abigail's face paled as she glanced up and down the street. "How did they know?"

He shook his head. "Maybe David or one of the others out in South Dakota figured out the make and model of my car. We'll have to rent something."

"Okay, I can get us to a rental place." She glanced around again, as if lost for a moment, then pointed in the opposite direction from the way they'd come. "If we catch the bus at the end of the block, that'll take us by an Enterprise…" She paused, her eyes losing focus as she stared up at the sky, then she nodded. "Yes, that should work."

"Sounds good."

As they started walking, a car turned onto the street in front of them. The hairs on Micah's arms prickled. Every muscle went taut as the tires squealed and the car careened down the street.

Heading right toward them.

NINE

Adrenaline flooded Micah's system as he watched the car speed down the street. As it approached, the vehicle slowed and the driver's window rolled down, revealing the barrel of a gun.

"Get down!" he yelled, sweeping Abigail to the ground. He winced as his knees and forearms hit the sidewalk, taking the brunt of the fall as he cocooned her in his arms.

And just in time. Gunshots rang out, taking out car windows and biting into the brick facades of the bungalows beyond them. As soon as the driver passed the parked cars, he'd have a clear shot.

Abigail pushed up onto her hands and knees, gesturing frantically at a wooden privacy fence running between the two nearest bungalows. "That way. An alley runs behind the houses."

"Go! Go!" He took off after her, keeping

himself between her and the car as it trundled down the street. More shots fired, kicking up bits of grass, dirt and splinters of wood where the bullets hit the fence ahead of them.

They ducked behind it and kept going, running for the back alley that allowed home-owners to access the detached garages behind the bungalows. At the back of the lot, the fence teed into the garage but there was no gate. Abigail skidded to a stop, glancing back at him, and he cupped his hands together and held them out.

She nodded, then stepped up onto his hands and he boosted her over the fence. After getting a running start, he hoisted himself over. There was no sign of the car in the alley yet, but it wouldn't take long for the driver to catch up.

Taking Abigail's hand, he tugged her forward into an all-out sprint up the side of the alley, dodging cars, trash cans, and faded plastic ride-on toys. They burst out onto the next street as police sirens echoed in the distance.

Abigail's eyes widened and she shook her head, gasping for breath. "We...don't... want..."

"The police to get us, I know." He glanced up and down the street. "Which way to the bus stop?"

They took off in the direction she indicated,

Micah only slowing the pace when she started to lag. Her face burned red and she was puffing for breath, but still she urged him onward. Finally, they spilled out of a side street onto a bigger road, one with four lanes of traffic and stoplights glowing red and green from here to infinity.

Vehicles chugged past slowly in the city traffic, releasing clouds of exhaust that made it even harder to breathe, especially for his not-yet-recovered lungs. He coughed violently, and Abigail shot him a worried glance.

"I'm fine," he choked out, then pointed at a glass and metal shelter a hundred yards away near a street corner. "Is that it?"

She nodded, wrapping a hand around his arm and pulling him forward. "I forgot how hard this must be on your lungs."

"Not like we had a choice. It was worth straining my lungs not to get killed." He winked at her, and a smile tugged at her lips.

At the sound of a large engine approaching, he glanced back over his shoulder. Never had the sight of a bus been more welcome.

"That's it," Abigail confirmed. They jogged the remaining distance to the bus stop, arriving just in time to flag down the driver. Micah paid their fares and they settled into seats, taking a long moment to catch their breath.

His lungs burned uncomfortably, but there was no denying God's hand in such perfect timing for the bus to arrive exactly when they needed it. Would Abigail see it that way?

As soon as he could manage breathing and talking, he said, "Talk about providential timing, huh?"

She nodded, pressing a hand to her chest. "Someone is definitely looking out for you."

"For you too," he said gently. "I know it might not feel this way, but God loves you with the same overflowing, inescapable love that He has for me. Actually, the Bible says it's the same love He has for His own Son, because He makes us His children through Jesus."

"I'd like to fully believe that. I really would." She blinked rapidly, then turned away. "But it's so hard when all these awful things keep happening to me."

He sighed, soul-deep, and ran a hand over his beard. "I know, I get it. Bad stuff happens to all of us in this fallen world. God doesn't promise life will be easy, but He does promise He'll be with us."

When she didn't answer, he let the subject drop and offered up a silent prayer instead. *Please, Lord, help her to see how much You love her.*

Watching her in pain like this made his

heart hurt, worse than he'd thought possible for someone he'd only met a week ago. How had his life gotten so intertwined with hers so rapidly?

And—the question he really didn't want to face—what was he going to do about it? Nothing had been right between them since he'd dumped all his childhood drama on her. He'd hurt her—maybe not as much by pushing her away as by stealing her chance at hope. She'd held out her fragile question to him, and he'd trampled it.

How could he spout all these promises about God and yet offer her no hope for relationships? Wasn't God sovereign over them too? Hadn't He been right there with Micah when his mother left? When he'd found out she was dead? When Taylor dumped him?

If God worked all things for the good, didn't that include all that horrible stuff? How could he keep telling Abigail about God's love when he wasn't fully accepting it himself?

The questions plagued him as they headed out of the car rental lot an hour later in a shiny silver Nissan, back to South Dakota and the promise of wrapping up this case.

Letting her go would be so much less messy. Safer. It had been the plan all along, and there was no reason to chuck that plan. But as he wrestled with his doubts, he couldn't shake the feeling he'd been lying to himself all along.

Abigail sat with her hands tucked beneath her legs, her handbag with its precious cargo resting securely against her feet. They'd crossed the border from Wisconsin into Minnesota about an hour ago, and the last dying rays of sunshine had faded from purple twilight into darkness.

Micah yawned again—he'd been doing it more frequently this last hour, despite the two-hour nap he'd taken while she drove out of Chicago and into Wisconsin. Sometimes the yawn would break off into more coughing, some of the spasms so strong her fingers edged toward the steering wheel. Just in case.

"Want me to take another turn driving?" she offered.

"No, I can hold out a little longer. You should try to sleep."

Ha, as if *that* was going to happen. Despite the fact every muscle in her body ached after the day they'd had, there was no way her mind was going to stop whirring. Not with all the revelations the day had brought. Eric's money tucked away in a Swiss account. The files. That list of names—everyone in the city Eric suspected as being in the mob's pay, with the little asterisks preceding those he could confirm.

Eric Fox.

She shuddered.

"What time did you say we're meeting the FBI agent?" she asked, just to keep herself thinking about something else.

"Brian had it set for tomorrow at four p.m., but I told him we're driving straight through so he's trying to get us in first thing in the morning. The office is in Rapid City."

"Good." She picked absently at her fingernails as her mind drifted again to those files. They felt like her ticket to freedom, to Owen and the life she wanted to rebuild, but what if she was wrong? "Do you think it will be enough? Or will they keep coming after me?"

"It'll be enough." Micah said it so matter-of-factly, she wished she could borrow some of his confidence. "A forensic accountant will have to verify everything, but from what I saw, your husband was very thorough. Once they arrest the people at the top, the underlings will leave you alone. And that list of names is going to trigger a whole chain of investigations and arrests."

He broke off, pausing to pass a semi-truck, then went on. "The list might even be more valuable than the files themselves. In fact,

Brian already forwarded the pictures I sent from my phone to the agent, though we'll have to go over everything with him again."

She nodded, even though he couldn't see her in the dark. That had been the first thing they'd done as soon as they left the city, before he'd dozed off in the passenger seat. While she navigated through the early rush-hour traffic, he'd patiently flipped through the entire file, snapping one photo after another and texting them to Detective Overton. Everything except the smaller envelope with the information about Eric's bank accounts. They'd wait to discuss it in person when they could speak to an IRS representative too.

Some of the tension eased in her chest. Eleanor had shared a video of Owen earlier in the day, sitting on a big horse, a giddy smile on his little face. He'd waved and yelled, "Hi, Mommy!"

Would she be able to reunite with him again soon? To be safe and quit running for their lives? After everything that had happened, it felt too good to be true.

"Abigail." Micah's voice interrupted her thoughts. He cleared his throat, shifting in his seat. "I owe you an apology. For all that stuff I said the other night, about how relationships always fail. The thing is, God's love and grace cover everything, and just because we've had bad experiences doesn't mean He can't bring good from them."

She straightened in her seat, warning bells going off in her mind. Where was he going with this?

"It's not honest of me to encourage you to trust His love and promises but not do that myself. I've been carrying the hurt from my mom's death, and from Taylor, for a very long time. And if God is who He says He is, He can redeem even the most painful situations."

Every cell froze and her body went rigid, on high alert. She'd longed all day for things to be set right between them, but now that the moment was here, it terrified her. What if he wanted more than friendship?

"Can you forgive me?" he finished, his voice low and rough.

Relief eased into her gut when he didn't mention that foolish kiss. "Of course," she breathed. "There's nothing to forgive. I owe you everything after what you've done for me and Owen."

She could hear, rather than see, him shaking his head. But instead of arguing, he asked, "What will you do once we hand the files over? Will you stay in Interior?"

Her mouth went dry. Did it matter to him?

Did she *want* it to? This shouldn't be so complicated. She'd met him only recently, and the arrangements in Interior had never been permanent. All of it had been solely for the sake of protecting Owen until she could figure out what to do. How had her feelings spiraled so out of control?

She swallowed. "Do you think it will be safe for me to get Owen? Or will they put me in witness protection? Will it take long to go to trial?"

"The FBI will jump all over this case." He paused, then went on, "I doubt you'll need witness protection, because the prosecution will hinge on these files, not on your testimony. Though they might want both of us to take the stand at some point."

She'd see him again? Her heart skipped, filling with obnoxious giddiness, before she squashed it back down.

"I...guess I don't know," she said carefully. "I could go out to Eleanor's until we know how things will proceed. There's no reason to keep the house in Interior." *Is there?* She hadn't realized until this moment how badly she wanted her choices to matter to him, and yet...

She couldn't go there. Not after what had happened with Eric.

"Going to your sister's would probably be

safest," he agreed, shifting his hands on the wheel. "I wouldn't recommend returning to Chicago until you get a green light from the authorities."

Disappointment wreathed her insides, mingling with a deflating sense of relief that left her even more confused. It was the answer she expected, the one she *wanted*—and yet his careful tone made something break inside her heart.

Foolishness.

They'd been thrown together out of necessity, and they certainly weren't going to become something more. No matter how much her stubborn heart wanted to consider that option. Out of the question.

She leaned her head back against the headrest and closed her eyes, slipping into an uneasy doze. Hours passed, until Micah finally pulled over at a rest area and agreed to let her take a turn driving.

Then more time slipped past in a blur of glaring headlights and green highway signs and stars twinkling overhead in the immense black sky, until the first rays of dawn cracked the inkiness in the east. When the giant signs for the World's Only Corn Palace came and went, and keeping her eyes open was a struggle, she pulled over at a rest stop.

Micah rotated in his seat, turning his head from one side to the other, but didn't wake. She pulled into a parking spot and cut the engine, hating to rouse him when he looked so peaceful. A strand of dark hair fell across his forehead, hanging over one of his eyes, and she reached over to brush it from his face. The move felt both natural and too intimate at the same time. Thankfully, he was asleep.

When his lips turned up into a slow grin and his eyes opened, she jerked her hand back. Heat flamed up the back of her neck. "Sorry, I… You had…" She shook her head. It all sounded stupid.

He blinked a few times, clearing the half-dazed look from his eyes, and sat up. "Where are we?"

"Rest stop about an hour and a half out, I think. My eyes were getting heavy." Not so much anymore, now that she'd made a fool of herself.

"I can drive." He inhaled a couple of deep breaths. "That nap really helped. Thanks."

"Any news from Detective Overton yet on the meeting time?" The sooner she could hand off these files, the better.

The interior cab lit up as he clicked his phone on and tapped in past the lock screen. "No…" His brows pulled together. "It's not like him to take this long to respond. Maybe he couldn't get ahold of the agent to confirm?"

"Should we head straight for the FBI office then?"

"No, his last text said he wanted to set it up somewhere else in Rapid City just in case they're monitoring the building. He was worried after I told him about the chase on the L and my car tires."

"Sure." She climbed out of the driver's seat, and after a quick restroom break, they swapped places.

They'd barely made it back onto the interstate when her cell phone rang. Micah stiffened, glancing at her, and her chest tightened. She'd only given the new number to a handful of people. Who would be calling at six in the morning?

"Maybe it's Brian calling you directly," he said.

She dug into her bag, pulling out the phone, then stared at the number. "It says 'unavailable' for the caller. Should I answer?"

"Yes. If the mob got ahold of your number, they don't need to call to track you."

She accepted the call and held the phone to her ear. "Hello?"

A strangled sob echoed through the line. "Abby?"

Her sister. "Els? What's going on? What's wrong?"

"They have us," Eleanor choked out between sobs, her voice catching on the words. "Owen and me. They have Owen."

The car's dashboard tilted in front of Abigail's eyes as the world dropped out from beneath her. *Please, God, no.* "But, I don't underst—"

She stopped as a man's voice muttered something in the background.

"He says you have three hours to bring the files, or…" She broke off into fresh tears, and Abigail's stomach corded up into knots.

She wanted to weep and scream at the same time, but she forced her voice to stay calm. "Eleanor, where are you? Give me anything. I'll get help."

"No, I can't, he won't—" Her sister stopped, then kept going after the man spoke in the background. "He says you have to come alone this time, Abby. Not like last time. He knows where you are."

David. It had to be David in the background, holding her sister and her son captive and spewing out those instructions. Rage burned inside her chest, making her want to throw the phone.

But that wouldn't save her family.

"Where?"

"He'll text you instructions on this number. You have three hours." Her sister's voice cracked. "Or they'll kill us."

"Owen, where is Owen?" Desperation edged into her voice, despite her efforts to stay calm. "Is he safe? Is he okay?"

The man's voice rose in the background, issuing more instructions. Telling Eleanor to hang up? Not without letting her know Owen was okay. A vise tightened around her ribs.

"He's asleep, he doesn't know. He—"

The line went dead.

Abigail stared at the phone in her hand, as if she could will it to come back on and undo that entire conversation. Or better yet, make all of this go away.

Instead, she inhaled deeply to counter her racing heart and turned to Micah, whose grim expression indicated he'd heard the entire conversation.

Even if it cost her life, or Eric's files, or his money in the Swiss bank, it didn't matter. Not compared to Owen.

She balled her hands into fists, nails digging into her palms, but she kept her voice steady.

"Micah, I have to save my son, and I have to go alone."

TEN

The first text arrived an hour later as the landscape shifted and the pale, sandy buttes of the Badlands exploded on the horizon like giant tombstones. Glaring sunlight burned the empty expanse of land. Micah gripped the steering wheel, his chest as hollow and empty as their surroundings, as Abigail read the message aloud. He'd tried to reason with her over how the authorities could help, but she'd stubbornly clung to her position.

He got it, he really did. Her son's and sister's lives were on the line. But in a situation like this, where they'd be witnesses to the men involved—where they'd already seen so much, in fact—the odds of any of them leaving alive weren't good. If the mobsters didn't want to kill them outright, all they had to do was abandon them somewhere in the remote wilds surrounding Rapid City. It wouldn't take long in this heat.

And after that conversation they'd had, where he'd come way too close to revealing how much he cared, his emotions were already a wreck. Thankfully he'd treaded carefully, waiting to see how she'd respond rather than plowing ahead. When she'd told him she'd be leaving Interior, he couldn't help but feel relieved he hadn't said more.

"It says…" She cleared her throat. "Take exit 131 and leave the ranger by the giant prairie dog." She glanced up at him. "That's it, all it says."

He let out a slow breath, his brain scrambling to come up with any plan that didn't involve letting Abigail wander off alone into David's hands. He'd already updated Brian, who was working to pull together a SWAT team on his end. But there wasn't much they could do at this point without more information. "He's got to be location-tracking your phone, so he'll be able to see whether or not you stop."

But would they be watching the roadside stop to see if he actually got out of the vehicle?

Or worse, would they have some ambush prepared? Other vehicles were bound to be there, getting an early start into the national park. Or stopping on their way elsewhere for a photo op with the giant roadside attraction.

"What if someone's waiting there?" Abigail's voice shook. "You're on their hit list now too."

"Yeah, I had the same thought." He tapped his fingertips on the steering wheel. "But I'm more worried about you and how we're going to track you. What if we pull over but I don't get out? I could hide in the back seat."

"No, it's too risky," she said. "If they're monitoring the parking lot, or if one of them saw you still in the car... We can't."

He glanced at a green mile marker as it flashed past. Ten miles, which meant not much time. David was smart. "Okay, then I'm making some calls."

Nick Langston, the chief ranger, was first in the queue. Since he was driving, he had Abigail initiate the call from his contacts then hand him the phone. Micah offered a silent prayer of thanks when Nick picked up after one ring. His explanation didn't take long, and when he clicked off, some of the tension had ebbed out of his shoulders.

"He's assembling a team, and he'll have someone at the Ranch Store to meet me." He offered a half-smile at the confused look on Abigail's face. "That's the tourist trap next to the giant prairie dog. Now we need Brian Overton again."

She tapped in his name and handed the phone over as it rang.

"Micah, what's up?" Brian asked. He sounded fully alert, like he'd spent the last hour drinking coffee and waiting for more information.

Micah relayed the instructions from the text and the chief ranger's response. "He's putting together a small tactical team of rangers so we can follow from a distance. If he can get someone up here in time, we'll give her a tracker to wear. As soon as we can get through to the phone company, we'll be able to track her phone's location too."

"What about a tracking app? Can you install one?"

"It's a burner to replace her personal one. No apps. We don't know how they got the number." How *had* they gotten her number? From the sheriff? Anger burned deep in his gut at the potential betrayal, but there'd be time later to pursue justice. "What about on your end? You didn't tell the sheriff's office, right?"

"Right. I went straight to my contact at Rapid City FBI and he's assembling a SWAT team as we speak. They'll be a little behind you because of the drive but we'll keep you posted. Should be there by the time she makes contact."

Relief coursed through his veins like soothing liquid, dousing some of the angry fire. By the time he hung up, they'd reached the first sign for Exit 131. Two miles to go.

He glanced at Abigail. "The SWAT team has to come from Rapid City. They're gonna be slow. Our rangers will be able to follow sooner, but you'll have to go slow. Drive the speed limit or even slower."

Her jaw flexed as she clenched her teeth. "But they have—"

He reached over and took her hand, squeezing it gently. "They have Owen. And your sister. I know. I know your gut is telling you to do whatever it takes to get to them as fast as humanly possible, but our goal is to extract all three of you *alive*. It won't help for you to rush in, hand over those files, and then get shot. Owen needs you alive as much as—" He gulped. "He needs his mother."

"But David said..." She frowned. "He won't let them go, will he?"

Micah shook his head. "Or you. You've seen too much. And then they'll track me down next, if there isn't already somebody waiting at that drop-off." He rubbed his thumb across the smooth skin of her knuckles, but she pulled away. Covered her mouth.

"I'm so sorry, Micah. I never should have dragged you into this."

"But none of that is going to happen, okay? We're going to track you to where they are, and the tactical teams will figure out how to get all three of you safely out of harm's way. That's why you need to stall as long as possible to give us time."

They'd reached the exit. Micah flipped on the turn signal and pulled over into the right lane, his heart rate accelerating as the car slowed.

"How will I know you're there?" Her voice was barely above a whisper as he slowed to a stop at the top of the off-ramp. No cars were coming, but he took his sweet time checking both directions before easing across the intersection to head south.

"You won't," he said grimly. "Not if we're doing it right. You'll have to trust us, that we know what we're doing. Have faith. You can always know that God is with you—He won't ever leave or forsake you."

Her throat bobbed as she stared straight ahead. Over the interstate, nice and slow, then a few miles south until the six-ton concrete prairie dog loomed on the right side of the highway. He turned into the parking lot, which held maybe half a dozen cars. A family posed in front of the prairie dog as they took a selfie. An older couple stood at one edge of the lot, staring at the mounds of sand dotting the prairie, waiting for one of the little rodents to pop up.

Micah pulled into a spot in the corner of the lot near the road. He cut the engine and slowly opened the door. Abigail got out on the passenger side.

Her brows pinched together as she glanced around the lot. "What's going to happen to you?"

"We'll find out." He squinted in the direction of the approaching car. It was hard to tell with the light glaring off it, but it *looked* like an NPS vehicle. If they could just get here in time with the tracker… He turned back to Abigail. "I'll be fine. I don't think they'll try anything here. It's too risky, not when what they really want is those files."

She swallowed. "You've got pictures, and so does Detective Overton. If anything happens to me, you can make sure the FBI gets them." She squinted at him. "But surely David expects that…?"

"He must think the originals will stand up better in court. Or that the defense attorneys

will be able to discredit the pictures." Or…
maybe he'd get Sheriff Layton to intervene
somehow. But Micah kept that last thought
to himself. No reason to frighten Abigail fur-
ther.

Her phone buzzed, and her face paled as
she read the message then held it up for him.

Get moving, now. If the ranger follows, the
game's up.

He crushed her against his chest, wishing
he could make this moment stretch for eternity. No more danger, no more old wounds or
broken hearts, just hope. His fingers tangled
in her silky hair. Then he released her and
looked down into her green gaze. "I'll see
you soon. No matter what, I'll come for you
and Owen and your sister. That's a promise."

"Thank you." Her mouth crumpled around
the edges. "I'm so glad you were buying groceries that day."

"Me too." Placing both hands on her head,
he pulled her close and kissed her forehead,
then stepped back. "Go now."

Ducking into the car, she slammed the driver's door shut and turned on the engine. He
stepped back, watching as she reversed the
car and turned out onto the main road head-

ing south. Toward his park. A stone dropped inside his chest as the car moved out of sight.

Where was his ride out of here? Every second mattered.

As he turned to look around, he saw something from the corner of his eye—a dark figure emerging from behind a parked car a few spaces away.

"I wouldn't go anywhere if I were you." The voice was painfully familiar.

Micah pivoted on one foot to face Vincenzo, who bore a lazy smirk on his smug face. The mobster held a gun in one hand, tapping it against his other palm in front of his stomach where only Micah could see it. No doubt trying to avoid the notice of anyone inside the store.

"See, the thing is," he said, "you wouldn't want to put anyone else in danger. It's my job to clean up any loose ends, and you're a loose end."

His pulse kicked up as the other man raised the gun. "So, what, you're just going to shoot me in broad daylight? You'll be joining your pals in jail before long."

Vincenzo shrugged, like he couldn't care less about their fate. "Only the stupid ones get caught. Now, I'll need you to hand over your phone and get in the car. We're going for a little ride."

His phone chimed. A text? He longed to glance down but wouldn't risk taking his attention off the other man. Engines rumbled past on the interstate in the distance, but was that the sound of one on the road? Surely Nick was on his way, if Micah could only stall a little longer.

"If we need to do this the hard way, we will," Vincenzo said. "Drop the phone. Now."

"Here, on the ground?" Micah pointed at the rough pavement. That phone held all their back-up photographs of the files, and right now it was his only connection to the rest of the team. He did *not* want to hand it over.

"That'll work just fine." Vincenzo raised the gun, angling his body so it wasn't visible from the store, or from where the family of tourists were now headed back to their car at the far end of the lot. "Unless you want me to shoot it out of your hand."

He lowered it slowly, bending at the waist and darting a glance toward the road to the south. Blinding sunlight glared off a windshield heading their direction—was that a hint of white on the front hood? *Please let it be Nick.*

"Drop it," Vincenzo growled, and Micah released the phone. It fell a foot and a half, hitting the pavement with a dull thud.

He flinched as Vincenzo fired the gun, and nearly simultaneously the phone exploded into a cloud of plastic and glass shrapnel that pelted off his pants and bit into his exposed arms.

Across the parking lot, raised voices echoed from the store's front porch, but Micah couldn't catch the words.

Vincenzo waved the gun at him. "Into the car now, or I shoot you right here."

Micah lifted his stinging hands and inched closer to the vehicle. The mobster backed his way around the front of the car, keeping the gun trained on him. If he dove for cover on this side, would it be enough protection at this range? He didn't dare glance at the main road to see if back-up was coming, but as he approached Vincenzo's car, he caught a glimpse of a reflection in the window glass.

A white SUV was slowing on the main road, its turn signal on, and praise the Lord, there was a green stripe running down the side. The driver kicked on the lights in a burst of red and blue, and the sirens screeched out across the parking lot. Relief coursed through him, but he wasn't safe yet.

Vincenzo swore, raising the gun, and Micah dove for the ground next to the car, crashing onto the hard pavement as shots rang out. The mobster jumped into the driver's seat and cranked the engine on as the ranger's SUV pulled into the lot.

Vincenzo threw his car into Reverse and backed up, then hit the gas. The car barreled forward, its engine revving.

Heading straight for Micah.

He lay frozen for a split second, then rolled to the left as the car bore down on him, landing on his side at the place where the asphalt met the edge of the prairie. A startled prairie dog chided him from a nearby hole before ducking back out of sight. His heart pounded like a jackhammer as he watched Vincenzo's car, waiting to see if the mobster would give up or swing the vehicle around.

But Nick was already in the lot, approaching fast, and the mobster was out of real estate. His car reached the end of the pavement and he kept going, bouncing over the grass and out onto the main road. Then he took off north, heading for the interstate.

The NPS vehicle pulled to a stop a few feet from Micah. The driver flung the door open and hopped out, leaving the engine idling.

Nick Langston jogged over, holding out his hand. "Micah, you all right?"

Micah groaned as he rolled onto his back and took the offered hand, letting the other man help him to his feet. "Yeah, I'm okay. Getting too old for this, though." He held out his arms, examining the tiny bits of what used to be his phone embedded in his skin.

"Looks like you need some medical attention."

He shook his head. "Not now." No amount of aches and pains would keep him from helping Abigail.

The chief ranger nodded toward the fleeing car, which was turning onto the I-90 West on-ramp. "We'll have to report the vehicle to the sheriff instead of chasing."

"Not sure that will do much good," he said grimly. At Nick's questioning look, Micah nodded toward the car. "I'll explain on the way."

As they climbed into the SUV, he asked, "What have we got?"

Nick buckled his safety belt and put the vehicle into Drive, heading for the road. "Two rangers gearing up at headquarters, and another two en route from Pinnacles Entrance. I told them to track but not intercept. Phone company's still working on the authorization but they're collecting the data. Should have it by the time we reach Ben Reifel."

Micah let out a tense breath through his teeth. The rangers coming from the Pinnacles wouldn't have the same tactical gear as the group from headquarters, but it was a smart move to have someone coming from the other direction. Depending on how far David intended Abigail to drive into the park, they might catch sight of her vehicle first.

He'd have to update Brian as soon as they had a lead on her location. "RCPD is working with the FBI field office to pull together a SWAT team, but they'll be a solid hour behind us."

Help was coming…but would it be enough?

Abigail clenched her hands around the steering wheel, fighting to keep her heart from pounding out of her chest. She could do this. For Owen and for Eleanor, she had to do this.

The park entrance stood just ahead, a green-and-black patch shimmering above the road in the growing heat. She slowed, keenly aware of Micah's absence as she fished for her wallet in her purse to pay the entrance fee. But as she approached, the ranger waved her through. The woman touched the brim of her hat, almost as if saluting her. Abigail swallowed, trying to keep the fear from choking her.

Micah or the chief ranger must have notified the others. How she wished she could pull over and wait for a team of them to join her, but David's instructions were clear.

She glanced at the phone again to see his latest text.

South into the park then west on Badlands Loop Road.

Would it be obvious which road she should take? Or if she went the wrong way and had to turn around, would he suspect her of picking up help?

The *what-ifs* spider-walked down her spine, setting each nerve on end. Driving the speed limit was painful, and every time the speedometer inched back up over forty-five mph, she took a deep breath and tried to relax her lead foot. Micah and the authorities needed that time to track her. Rushing headlong into danger wouldn't help Owen—but even knowing the facts couldn't completely stop her instincts.

Minutes felt like hours as she crawled around one bend after another, majestic buttes and spires passing in a blur of beige against a harsh blue sky. There was the Visitor Center and park headquarters on her right, its roof blackened and partially collapsed in the back, blocked off with construction tape. A physical marker of the trauma she and Micah had endured these past few days. Opposite the Visitor Center, a road branched off to the right, identified by a sign reading *Badlands Loop*.

That had to be it. She made the turn, praying that somewhere back at headquarters a team was mobilizing to help her. Micah's words came back to her—about how God would never abandon her or leave her to face life's troubles alone.

Have faith, he'd said. Her throat burned, and she sucked in a quivering breath. Not being alone would be really nice right now. How could she have faith God was with her when she *felt* so alone?

But she wasn't truly alone, not if Micah was right. He'd been beaten up by life, the same as her, yet he still had such beautiful faith. Was it possible God had been there all along for her too, only she hadn't been looking? He didn't have to send Micah to help her that first time David took Owen, but He had. Maybe He would be with her now too if she asked. She'd been doing a lot of blaming lately and not much asking.

The thought hit like a punch in the stomach. Tears sprang into her eyes, blurring her vision. *I'm sorry, God. Please forgive me for not trusting You. Be with me now. Help me to know You're here.*

Gentle warmth wrapped around her soul like a cozy blanket on a rainy day, and she had the distinct impression He'd heard her prayer. That He was with her, and that no matter what happened, He wouldn't abandon her. She sat up a little straighter, loosening her grip on the steering wheel. Relaxing into His grace and His strength. She'd carried the burdens of her marriage and Eric's choices and the awful fallout all alone for so long, but that wasn't God's plan, was it? He'd never asked her to handle everything by herself.

A familiar Bible verse pressed upon her heart. *Come unto me, all ye that labor and are heavy laden, and I will give you rest.* That was what God offered her—His peace, His help, His presence—as she faced life's hardships. Not a promise that there wouldn't *be* hardships. She'd wasted so many years trying to handle everything on her own, when she had this amazing promise from her Creator.

His peace and comfort filled her heart as the miles passed in a blur of multicolored buttes and green prairie grassland. Just a tiny fraction of the beauty of God's handiwork. She wasn't sure how far she'd gone when her phone vibrated again.

South on 509. Park at the picnic area on the right.

She scanned the road as she rounded a bend. The left turn for Route 509 was just ahead, not more than a few hundred yards. A chill swept over her and the hairs on her arms stood on end. David knew exactly where she was.

A few minutes later, a parking lot appeared on the right. Wooden picnic tables covered with slatted shades dotted the landscape beyond it. She turned in and pulled into a spot, her muscles twitching from adrenaline overload. Other than her vehicle, the lot was empty. Where was David? And how did he plan to get away once he had the files?

As soon as she cut the engine, her phone pinged with a new text.

Deer Haven trail. Bring the files.

She glanced at her handbag, debating whether to carry just the manila envelope or bring the entire bag. If she was walking to her death, would it matter? She yanked the big envelope out and stuffed the bag as far as she could under the seat. At least that way Micah would have the letter with Eric's bank account information if anything happened to her. When the dust settled, if the authorities didn't repossess the funds, he could pass it along to Eleanor or her parents for Owen.

Because Owen was going to be fine.

Her jaw ached as she climbed out of the car, and she took a slow breath, releasing some of the tension from clenching her teeth. It was close to 9:00 a.m. now, and the sun was already baking the barren ground. The air tasted bitter and dusty against her tongue, making her long for a drink of water. But the bottle she'd picked up at a rest area hours ago was long empty, and there was nothing she could do about it now.

After shutting the car door and locking it, she skirted the edge of the parking lot until she reached the trailhead. A backcountry registration box was mounted on a post, along with warning signs about "no potable water" and "beware of rattlesnakes." She glanced down at her exposed ankles above her canvas flats and grimaced.

The path gleamed white against prairie grasses growing on either side. To the left and right, the layered buttes of the Badlands rose skyward nearby. The going was easy at first, winding in and around spurs of textured rock as the path cut through the only traversable route. The way the sediments had deposited in such distinct layers, each their own shade of tan or brown or pink, was fascinating. Maybe one day she'd learn how this terrain was formed.

If she lived that long.

Her tongue felt like a dry wad of cloth and her forehead grew slick with sweat by the time she'd walked for half an hour. At least there hadn't been any telltale rattling sounds. Maybe it was hot enough that the snakes would be hiding in their holes. Up ahead, the landscape shifted, the buttes giving way to prairie grassland to the south. To the north, the trail clung to the natural curve of the Badlands, vanishing from view. Something moved far off in the distance out on the grassland—too big to be a hiker. Bison?

Her phone pinged.

Leave the trail around the next bend. Fifteen paces back between the twin spires.

Did that mean Owen was close? Her heart rate quickened. Far away to the east, a thin ribbon of black looked like it might be the road she'd left behind. Definitely not a river. On her right, a butte rose a hundred feet into the air, its sides steep and pitted from centuries of water runoff.

She picked up her pace almost unconsciously, half-jogging, until she remembered what Micah had said. Going slowly would give the team more time to catch up to her. But forcing her feet back into a walk was nearly impossible when she was so close.

David had said around the next bend. She clutched the envelope tighter as she skirted the southern end of the butte on her right. Hair blew into her face as a light breeze from the west kicked up, and she brushed it aside. The air smelled of sand mixed with the subtle sweetness of grass, and she couldn't shake the stubborn feeling of hope that somehow everything would be all right.

But when she passed the end of the butte, and the space beyond opened into a narrow passage of sandy earth to the right, a knot formed in her stomach. Rising at the back of the gap between this butte and the next were the two spires, shrouded in shadow.

There was no turning back.

ELEVEN

The place was eerily silent as Abigail picked her way across the uneven ground toward the twin spires. Wind rustled the long prairie grasses behind her, but between the arms of the tall buttes the air was still as a tomb. She glanced again at the instructions on the phone. Fifteen paces. She hadn't remembered to count. Did it matter?

Tension squeezed her chest as she kept going. A cascade of tiny rocks rolled down a slope somewhere close by, nearly making her jump out of her skin. She strained to hear any sign of a little boy's voice, but there was nothing. The invisible band around her ribs tightened. What if it had been a trick? What if Owen and Eleanor were being held somewhere else, and this was all a wild goose chase just to get the files out of her?

She forced in an unsteady breath. *Please protect them, Lord. Only You can take care of us right now. I trust You and Your plan.* Just thinking the words helped ease some of the anxiety clawing at her insides, even though every muscle stayed on high alert.

Movement flashed ahead and she froze mid-step. With the grating sound of footsteps on sand, a man with a bushy mustache appeared from behind one of the big spires. He held a small gun in one hand and braced himself with the other as he navigated the uneven terrain. She didn't recognize him, but he waved her forward.

"This way," he grunted. As she approached, he held out his empty hand and pointed at the phone she still clutched in one hand. "I'll take that. You won't need it anymore."

She squeezed her palm around the hard metal, then held it out. The man's cold eyes never left hers as he took it out of her hand and held the power button. Her mouth went dry. Would they still be able to track it if it was shut off? He turned and pulled his arm back then hurled the phone as far as he could out into the prairie. She watched the arc of the small black lump until it vanished into the grass. If Micah could track her this far, it would be close enough, wouldn't it? *Please, Lord.*

"Let's go." The man waved the gun at her, gesturing toward the spires.

She dragged her gaze away from the place the phone had fallen and started forward, picking her way over rocks as she climbed between the two narrow tower formations. On the other side, she stepped out into a maze of the Badlands—curving buttes, towering spires, and jagged pinnacles. Her heart sank. How would Micah ever find them here? She couldn't exactly leave a trail of breadcrumbs for him to follow.

Something sharp nudged her back. "Get moving," the man snapped. "We got a ways to go, and it's already boiling out here."

If she just had a little more time, maybe she could think of some clue to leave to indicate which direction they were going. "Is my little boy okay?" she asked, hoping the man wouldn't notice how slowly she was moving.

"For now," the man growled, and a shudder rippled down her spine. "No, that way," he ordered after a few minutes, directing her to the right when the path split around an odd-shaped tower of rock.

What had Micah told Owen about the rock here? That it had been shaped by wind and rain because *it was soft*. She scanned the ground, frantically looking for anything hard or sharp. Something bleached white from the sun jutted from the side of the path. From the oddly curved shape, it almost looked like part of an animal's jawbone.

Ordinarily she'd be disgusted, but not today. Instead, she let a toe snag on the ground and crashed down in what she hoped looked like an accidental fall. Her fingers curled around the jaw fragment as the man grunted something. As she scrambled to her feet, she tucked the bone against her left palm and swiped it against the rock spire. There was no way to look back, to make sure she'd left a decent mark. Nothing to do but pray that someone would follow her trail and notice it.

At each junction of the trail, she did the same, pretending to brace herself against the rock while digging in that scrap of bone. *Please, God, let it be enough.* It didn't take long to become thoroughly disoriented. The sun hadn't peaked yet, so she had a vague idea which way was east, but they'd taken so many turns weaving through the rock formations, she'd never find her way out on her own.

Hopefully it wouldn't come to that. *Please let Micah find us*, she prayed silently. He was out there somewhere close by, tracking her down. The phone company would at least lead them to the trailhead, and the rangers knew this land far better than she did. Or the mobsters.

Her thoughts turned to her son. Her family. Micah… The thought of not seeing them again opened a black hole inside her stomach.

She'd make it.

She had to.

The other rangers were ready by the time Nick pulled the SUV into the parking lot next to the Ben Reifel Visitor Center. Micah grimaced when he saw the yellow caution tape cordoning off the back quarter of the building, and the closed sign plastered across the entrance. He hadn't seen the full extent of the damage the night of the fire, not with the injuries he'd sustained from the smoke.

The chief ranger left the engine idling as he and Micah jumped out to greet the other two rangers. Andre and Rachel jogged out from a staff entrance, wearing protective vests over their uniforms and carrying extra sets, which he and Nick quickly put on. One of them handed him a medical kit.

"What'd you get out of Verizon?" Nick asked Rachel.

The older woman pointed west. "They tracked the phone out on Badlands Loop

Road, south on 509, and stopping at Conata picnic area. The signal hasn't moved."

Micah exchanged a glance with Nick. "That means our other team is closer."

The chief ranger nodded. "I'll notify them to ID the vehicle and look for suspects, but not to engage unless absolutely necessary."

He prayed it wouldn't come to that. "What's our approach?" It didn't seem likely David would arrange a meeting right there in the parking lot. More likely, they'd use the terrain to stay hidden. But then why hadn't Abigail's phone moved?

A vision of the phone lying abandoned—or worse, lying on the ground next to Abigail's body—ripped through his brain. He braced a hand against the SUV to steady himself.

"We'll get the report from the other team," Nick said, "then make the call. Most likely we'll park to the north using the terrain as cover."

Focus on the job, Ellis. Thinking about worst-case scenarios didn't do any good. He climbed back into the SUV's front passenger seat as the other rangers loaded into the vehicle. As Nick turned the vehicle out of the lot and headed for Badlands Loop Road, Micah tapped in Brian's number on Nick's phone.

The phone rang, once, twice, then went

to voicemail. Micah took his frustration out on his teeth, then unclenched his jaw long enough to leave a message. He shared the coordinates for Abigail's phone from the Verizon operator and provided an update on the ranger teams' locations.

He clicked off, half-expecting a return call any second, but none came. Where was Brian? Tied up with the rest of his team? Or had he ignored the call because it wasn't Micah's number?

He pulled a pair of tweezers out of the medical kit and set to work on the shrapnel in his arms. Even with Nick pushing the speed limit, the road was winding, slow and long, and every minute brought Abigail closer to facing David and the other mobsters. And her sister and Owen... Thinking about the little boy tugged at the places deep inside he'd closed off, filling his chest with a sweet ache.

Have I been wrong this whole time, Lord? Was it possible that the joys of family and healthy relationships could outweigh the risks of rejection and heartbreak? Here he stood, on the brink of losing this woman and her child he cared so much about, despite every effort to guard his heart. And she didn't even know how much he truly cared.

"You okay?" Nick asked.

His friend glanced at him and Micah swallowed, trying to put some moisture back in his dry mouth. "Just praying we get there in time."

"She means a lot to you." The chief ranger said it as a statement rather than a question, like it was obvious to everyone. Micah glanced back at the others in the rear, but they were speaking to each other in low tones.

He dragged a hand through his hair. When he made eye contact with Nick again, he nodded. Sometimes words weren't necessary.

"We'll get there in time," Nick said, then turned his focus back to the wheel, picking up the pace just a bit.

A few minutes later, a call came through on Nick's radio. The other team had circled past Conata and found the rental car. It was the only vehicle in the lot.

"How are they planning to get away?" Micah exchanged a glance with Nick, who shook his head. There weren't many options out here, short of all-terrain vehicles or a helicopter. "Unless they've got a ride coming…" Vincenzo?

"Copy," Nick replied on the radio. "Any sign of either suspects or hostages?"

The radio crackled. "Negative. Should we commence the search on foot?"

"Negative. Wait for us. ETA ten minutes. Langston out."

A weight settled in Micah's gut. They must have taken Abigail into the network of buttes, with its impassable cliffs and towering pinnacles and hidden crannies. It was unforgiving territory, and she was with dangerous men. *God, keep her safe. Please.*

How would they find her in time?

Abigail followed the man deeper into the maze of the Badlands, doubts and fears assailing her with each step, until they rounded a bend into a shadowy crevice, and he ordered her to stop. A sound reached her ears, carried on the breeze above the still air between the walls of rock, and her heart leaped. Too high-pitched to be an adult—it had to be Owen. He was out here, just like David had said. Longing swept over her, buckling her knees. Her arms had never felt so empty.

"Is that—"

Before she could finish the question, something moved in the shadows deeper in the crevice. She stiffened as a man stepped out into the light, an ugly sneer plastered across his face beneath windblown blond hair. *David.*

"Nice to see you again, Abigail." He stuffed

both hands into his pockets and leaned casually against one of the rock walls a few feet away.

She hugged the envelope to her chest. It was hard to believe she and Eric had ever trusted him. "Where's my son?"

David cocked his head to one side. "What about your poor sister? She doesn't count?"

"She's an adult. Owen is a child. He should never have been involved in this."

"And you should've given us what we wanted in the first place," David snarled. "It never would've come to this."

"I didn't know what you wanted!" A righteous sob worked its way up her throat. "You should be ashamed of yourself."

"Shut up!" He jerked his head at the man behind her, who jabbed her with the gun. The barrel felt cold and hard against her back. "Might I remind you, there's nothing preventing me from killing you right now?"

Anger flared beneath her ribs, fiery hot and strong, driving out the fear that had made her knees weak for far too long. "Eric trusted you. *I* trusted you. And you betrayed us. You think you'll get away with it, but you won't. Even if you kill me and take this evidence and destroy all of it, the mafia doesn't care about you. As soon as you're a liability, they'll take you out too. And some day you'll answer to God for what you've done."

David's eye twitched as he stood stock-still for a fraction of a second. Then he shifted his weight and yawned, the movement stiff and forced. "Are you done with your little sermon? Because I need those files before I can reunite you with your family. Owen is fine, by the way. He and your sister are exploring the terrain right over there while you and I have our little chat. That kid sure asks a lot of questions."

Abigail narrowed her eyes. David hadn't earned the right to say anything about her son. But provoking him wouldn't help this situation end better, and Micah had told her to stall. So she swallowed her angry thoughts and forced in a slow breath.

She tapped the envelope with one of her hands. "Before I hand these over to you, I want to know something. How did Eric get involved with the mob? Were you the one who referred the clients to him?"

"And now *you're* asking questions too." He sighed and tipped his face skyward, silent for several seconds. "Look, Abigail, I didn't mean for it to happen." When he returned his gaze to her, he couldn't quite make eye contact. "When you first moved to Chicago,

I was clean. I just wanted to reconnect with a friend. But once I realized what I'd gotten involved in, and they demanded referrals..." His jaw tightened, the faint look of regret she'd glimpsed gone now. "The pay is excellent, and if you're smart... It didn't have to turn out this way. I tried to warn him."

"Wait." She paused, trying to absorb his last words. "You warned Eric? You knew what he intended to do?"

"He told me he wanted out. I patiently explained it wasn't an option. Not in this lifetime, anyway. But he insisted he could do it. That he had evidence stashed away that could lock up the *don* for life."

David's eyes grew hard as glittering amber gemstones, and suddenly the truth hit Abigail like a punch to the stomach. "You turned him in, didn't you? You were the one who told the mob about the files."

He laughed bitterly. "I'm surprised it took you this long to figure it out."

"Did you shoot him too?"

"No, that wasn't me. But I arranged a meeting at Eric's office that morning and let the hitman inside the building. When Eric wouldn't tell us where the files were, we searched the office."

Her stomach churned. She *knew* it wasn't a

suicide. Whatever bad mistakes her husband had made, he hadn't deserved what David did to him. "Did you watch him die?"

"Of course not." He shook his head. "Stop being so dramatic. No sense in sticking around to risk getting caught. The mob's hit-men know exactly what they're doing."

If only Micah and the SWAT team would appear right now. Sweep in over the tops of those formations behind David and arrest him. Then they'd get him on the stand and he could prove that Eric was killed. Her husband would be vindicated on at least *some* level.

But only the faint sounds of Owen's voice carried on the breeze from somewhere nearby, interspersed with her sister's deeper tones. No hint that rescuers were on the way. Fear edged back into her stomach, curling tendrils around her insides and unraveling some of the strength she'd felt while focusing on her anger.

"Why do you keep looking around?" David asked, taking a step closer. The musky scent of his cologne took her instantly back to the Walmart parking lot where he'd taken Owen. Panic spiked her insides, and she wrapped her fingers tighter around the envelope to keep them from shaking. "If you're hoping for rescue, it's not coming in time. Not for you, anyway. I suppose your sister and son will have a chance, once we turn them loose. If they can survive that long without water."

"So that's your plan?" Her voice came out an octave too high, and she forced herself to stand straighter. "Shoot me? And leave them here in the desert to die?"

He shrugged. "Pretty much. I'd leave you to die with them, but I can't run the risk of you somehow finding your way back out." His gaze drifted to the envelope pressed against her chest like a shield. "Of course, if you don't hand over the files, we can just shoot all three of you." He held out his hand, waggling his fingers.

Abigail gritted her teeth. "You promise you'll let them go?" Not that his word meant *anything*. Or that she had any bargaining chips left.

"Sure." He jerked a thumb over his shoulder. "Peter, up there on guard, is just waiting on word from me and then we'll be on our way."

With a rough sigh, she relaxed her death grip on the files and held the envelope out. He snatched it from her hand, tore it open, and thumbed through the pages without removing them. The smile he offered almost looked like the old David for a minute, the man they'd invited over to dinner and gone to Cubs games with. His shoulders slumped for just a second, as if in relief, and then he turned to the man behind her.

"Wait five minutes, till I'm over the top. I don't want to watch."

Her stomach plunged into her toes as she glanced between him and the other man, who lifted his gun. "Now?" She hated the way her voice shook. "Owen will hear."

David turned away and started climbing up the rock wall behind him, toward the top of the formation, without looking back.

The man in front of her raised his gun, a slow, cruel smile spreading across his face. "Then I suggest you don't scream."

Where is she? Where is she?

The thought ran like a mantra through Micah's head as he scrambled up a rock formation, loose gravel giving way beneath his hands and feet. Grit coated his face and sweat poured down his back beneath the flak jacket. With the sun scorching down as it drew higher in the sky, it had to be over ninety degrees already. And it was only ten in the morning.

They'd parked north of the lot, hiding the vehicles off-road, and given equipment to the pair of rangers from Pinnacles. Without an exact trace on Abigail's location, they'd split up to cover more area. Micah had found her phone out in the grassland next to a prairie dog den—thrown aside, as he'd suspected, not far from the start of the trail. A handful of backpackers had logged in at the trailhead, but no one had called in a report of suspicious activity. Deer Haven trail skirted the southern edge of the Badlands for a few miles before turning north, and anyone walking its path would be easily visible from the south. It wasn't likely the mobsters would risk being seen.

Which meant they'd taken her off trail, into this vast network of jagged dried mud sculpted by God millennia ago. He crested the ridge and paused, keeping low to the ground, listening for any indication of where she might be. Scanning the landscape ahead for any clue.

Wait—along the side of that spire, where the path diverged just ahead...

He slid down the other side of the ridge and jogged over to the spot, rubbing a finger along a mark in the rock. Fresh dust came off on his skin. Someone had carved this recently. His heart ballooned with hope. *Abigail?*

He took the junction on the side of the

mark, his gaze roving the rocky landscape for more carvings. There, another one, to the left at the next spire.

Please, Lord, let me get to her in time.

Soft murmuring carried on the breeze, and he quickened his pace. That sounded a whole lot like voices. His equipment felt too loud, like everything rattled and *thunked* as he moved, following the trail of marks on the rock.

The sound was coming from just ahead, between those two arms of a butte. He paused to check the coordinates on his handheld GPS communicator, then shared the information with the team. The others would head for this location.

Cautiously he edged forward. A pinnacle jutted out at the base of the nearest arm, creating a gap in the rocky outcropping. He wiped his sweaty palm on his pants and tightened his grip on his gun, hardly daring to breathe as he inched closer.

"He'll let them go, won't he?" The strain in Abigail's voice made his heart ache. Was she talking about Owen and her sister? Were they with her?

Whoever was there didn't answer.

He reached the pinnacle and pressed against the rock, his cheek brushing its gritty surface as he strained to see into the gully. Part of a man's left shoulder was visible around the bend of rock. From this angle he could barely see in—he'd have to get closer.

Each movement felt too loud as he edged his way around the outside of the pinnacle, keeping as close to the rock as he could get. Face pressed against it, he leaned around the edge until a man's back came into view.

The man tipped his head sideways, glancing down at a wristwatch, and Micah's heart beat double-time as he pulled back before the man noticed him. The man's other arm was hidden from view, but there was no question he held a gun. After a moment, Micah held his breath and dared to lean around the edge again. In the shadows beyond the man, pressed against one of the rock walls like she could disappear into it, stood Abigail. Her face was pale, and her arms hugged her chest.

His gut reaction was to burst out and rescue her, but there might be more armed men. The safest scenario was to wait for backup. He kept his hand braced against the rock and scanned the tops of the butte above Abigail's head. No sign of movement up there, but was that a faint hint of voices beyond?

The man glanced at his watch again.

"That's five minutes," he grunted. "Any final words? Not that I'm gonna remember to pass them along." He laughed, the harsh sound echoing off the gully walls.

Micah's heart shot into his throat and every nerve fired on high alert as the man raised his other arm. Waiting for backup was no longer an option.

He stepped out from behind the cover of the rock formation, gun trained on the man's back. "Freeze!" he ordered. "Hands up where I can see them."

The man stiffened, and Micah held his breath as the man hesitated for a split second. Then he slowly lifted his arms over his head, pointing the gun up toward the sky. Behind him, Abigail sagged backward against the rock wall, hands still over her heart.

Good, the man was cooperating. But he wasn't out here alone, and it was only a matter of time before more guns showed up. He had to get Abigail to safety.

"Turn around, nice and slow," Micah ordered. "Abigail, back away from him and keep to the right." The space was too narrow for her to pass the man and stay safely out of his reach, but he wanted as much space between them as possible. Especially if he ended up having to shoot.

The man pivoted slowly, still holding the gun.

Sweat collected on Micah's forehead, dripping down to his eyebrows. Too many things could still go wrong. *Lord, now would be a good time for backup.* "Real slow," he said, "put the gun down and kick it over to me."

The man scowled but bent slowly toward the ground, lowering the gun.

"Alberto!" a familiar male voice called from above. The man who'd taken Owen— David. "What's the holdup?"

Every muscle went taut as David appeared on the top of the butte ten feet above where Abigail stood.

"You," David snarled. He drew his weapon and raised it.

There was no time to think, not with two against one. Micah lifted his arms, aimed for David's hip, and squeezed the trigger at the same moment David fired. Gunshots echoed against the rocks, blending with Abigail's scream. David's shot went wide, hitting the pinnacle to Micah's right and creating a spray of dried mud and debris.

Up above, David cried out and collapsed, but at nearly the same instant, something pummeled into Micah's chest with enough force to send him careening backward until he crashed into a slab of rock behind him.

"Micah!" Abigail screamed.

He couldn't breathe beneath the throbbing, crushing pain in his chest, but there was no blood—the flak jacket had seen to that. Horror ripped through his insides as Alberto pivoted on his heel, facing Abigail. She had wedged herself into the place where the two arms of the butte joined, but now there was nowhere to go as Alberto pointed his weapon at her.

Micah groaned, forcing his gun up despite every muscle in his upper body screaming in protest. His hands shook so violently there was no way to aim accurately, so he pointed to the man's left, away from where Abigail stood to the right.

He fired. The shot went left, hitting the rock and spewing dust into the air. But it was enough to get Alberto's attention. The man turned, and Micah fought with his body to hold his arms still. But his chest ached so badly he could scarcely keep the gun up, much less hold it steady.

And the other man knew it. A slow smile spread across his face as he raised his gun, this time aiming for Micah's head.

The shot rang out and someone screamed again. Micah waited for the blinding pain, the flashes of light, the darkness that would usher him into the Lord's presence, but none of it came.

Instead, the other man crumpled to the ground.

Micah slumped back against the rock, blinking to clear his vision. Men appeared on the butte above dressed in flak jackets like his—*thank You, God*. His team had found them.

A sob ripped from Abigail's chest as she ran toward him and stumbled to her knees next to his side. He gazed up at her, struggling to pull in decent breaths over the pain, as she examined his chest to find the injury.

"Flak…jacket…" he huffed out.

She ran both hands over the thick black fabric and nodded, biting her lower lip. Tears welled in the corners of her eyes. He had the sudden urge to kiss them away, but that was… No. He couldn't do that. He wasn't thinking clearly with all this pain.

"Mommy?" Owen's small voice rang out from the left, where he stood in the sparse grass with Abigail's sister and the chief ranger.

Abigail's green eyes met his for a second. She clapped a hand to her mouth then turned. "Owen, baby!" When she held out her arms, Eleanor let go of Owen's hand and he ran over to Abigail, throwing his small hands around the back of her neck.

Nick walked over with Eleanor and knelt on Micah's other side. His forehead crinkled as he scanned Micah's chest. "Looks like you took quite a hit."

"Great timing. You get the others?"

"Yeah, there was one man guarding these two." He tipped his head toward Eleanor and Owen. "Andre's got him. And you took down the ringleader up there."

Andre appeared in the direction Nick had come, hauling a cuffed mobster. Up on the butte, the other two were cuffing David. Nick got up and checked on Alberto but shook his head. "Didn't make it."

Micah sat up, wincing as his pectoral muscles objected. "What about the SWAT team? Where are they?"

"No word yet." The chief ranger frowned.

With Abigail and Nick's help, Micah made it to his feet. Owen ran up to him, a huge smile on his face.

He stood in front of him, hands clasped together shyly, then lunged forward and hugged Micah's legs. "Mr. Micah!"

Warmth bloomed in Micah's chest as he ruffled the boy's hair. "Hey, Owen!"

"I missed you so much, Mr. Micah! Auntie Eleanor has a horse named Theo and she let me ride him and we had ice cream three times and—"

"Let Mr. Micah talk to the other grown-ups now, sweet pea," Abigail said, scooping the little boy up. Her gaze met his over Owen's head, and the smile curving her lips made it suddenly hard to think about anything other than how beautiful she was.

"Come on," Nick said, "let's get you all back to the road and get some water. It's hot out here." He turned to Micah. "You okay to walk? Or do you want to wait for help?"

"Oh no, I'm coming with you." He'd have one monstrous bruise underneath the jacket, but his injuries weren't as pressing as getting those files to the FBI.

"What happened with the envelope?" he asked Abigail.

She bit her lip as a worried look flitted across her face. "I gave it to David."

"Here," Rachel said, handing it to Micah. "Was this what you're looking for? Found it up there." She nodded toward the top of the butte.

"Thanks." He gripped the envelope firmly in one hand and used the other to keep his balance as they navigated over the uneven terrain back to the trailhead. With the hit David had taken to his pelvis, he'd been unable to walk, so they'd left two of the rangers behind with him to wait on a medical evacuation.

A lone Rapid City police cruiser idled in the distance, and as they approached the parking lot, the driver cut the engine and jumped out.

"Brian?" Micah called as his friend jogged up to them. "What happened? Why are you alone?"

Brian pressed both hands to his face. "Micah, thank goodness you're all right. Your team is okay? You caught them?" He glanced over their group, his eyes lingering on the lone man in cuffs, the body wrapped in an emergency tarp, and finally stalling on the envelope in Micah's hand.

"Yeah, we caught them, but where's the SWAT team?"

He shook his head. "You're not gonna believe this—well, maybe you will—but Layton called them off. Told Hodgson it wasn't my jurisdiction, and his office would handle it." His lips pressed together as he glanced around. "But obviously his idea of 'handling it' was doing nothing. You're right. They must have gotten to him."

Micah glanced at the man they'd caught, but his face remained expressionless, leaving no hint as to whether he knew about an inside connection.

"So, I came alone," Brian went on. "Just pulled in. I'll get those files back to Hodgson myself, and we'll take care of this mess once and for all."

Nick rubbed a hand over his face. "We don't have prison cells in the park. We've got to take this one to the sheriff's department for processing, and we'll have to wait on an evac for the other. We can't bypass Layton and go to RCPD without causing a ruckus, regardless of what you suspect."

"What about the other two who wouldn't talk?" Micah asked Brian. "They're still locked up, aren't they? Or did Layton find some way to release them?"

"Far as I know, he's still got them. I can find out for you, but first priority is those files." He pointed at the envelope. "And Abigail's testimony. The sooner we get that to the FBI, the better."

He had a point, especially with Vincenzo still on the loose. Micah turned to Nick. "Permission to escort her?"

"You need medical care, Micah." The chief ranger glanced at Abigail, Owen, and Eleanor. "So do they. First stop should be the hospital."

Abigail kissed Owen and handed him to

her sister, then gently tugged at the envelope in Micah's hand. "I'll go with Detective Overton. You can follow with my sister and Owen. Detective Overton can take me to the hospital to meet you as soon as we're done at the FBI field office."

His fingers brushed against hers where they rested on the thick paper. The contact, though incidental, sent a jolt of electricity burning up his arm. "You sure about this? We can go together."

She rested her other hand against his chest, where the bullet would have penetrated his heart if not for the jacket. "I need to end this, Micah. You could have died today." Her eyes glistened, and she blinked rapidly. "So could my sister and my son." Going up on tiptoe, she pressed a soft kiss to his cheek right above the whiskers of his beard.

He wanted to take her in his arms, hold her close, and never let her go, but instead he nodded. She was the one who'd been through all of this mess—it was her decision to make. "All right. See you soon."

She took the envelope, handed him the keys to the rental, and climbed into the passenger seat of Brian's patrol car. He stood watching for a moment as they pulled out, then mustered his energy to get Eleanor and Owen into the rental car. Watching her drive off had hurt far more than it should. After all, wouldn't he be doing that again for keeps, now that they'd found the files? She and Owen would pack up their things and leave forever, and he'd be stuck here, left behind, watching them go.

Doing nothing about it because he was too...

Too what?

Afraid.

The thought hit him smack between the eyes. "Guarding his heart" and "protecting himself" sounded noble, but they were just euphemisms for fear. He'd been a coward, all because he didn't want to get hurt again.

But didn't this hurt just as much? Even more than what Taylor had done. She'd injured his pride, made him feel humiliated and foolish, but had she truly broken his heart? Not with this kind of pain.

He pressed a hand to his chest, massaging the growing bruise above his heart. At least physical injury he could deal with, but this...

What do I do, Lord?

He helped Eleanor and Owen into the car, letting the question simmer in the back of his mind, then climbed in behind the wheel. Nick and Rachel had already started across the parking lot with the cuffed suspect when suddenly Nick came jogging back.

He was out of breath by the time he stopped next to the car. Micah unrolled the driver's side window and shot him a puzzled glance as Nick held out his cell phone. "You need to hear this. Fred Hodgson, FBI field office. He called me. You can take my SUV."

Micah frowned. What was going on? "This is Ranger Micah Ellis."

"Ranger Ellis, Special Agent Hodgson, Rapid City office. I called to notify Chief Langston that we got a tip there might be organized crime members operating in the park. Wanted to give you a heads-up."

What? Either his injury was worse than he'd thought, or something was very seriously wrong. "But Detective Overton already spoke with you. He told you we'd be bringing evidence that could be used against the mafia. Abigail Fox's case? He was working to arrange a meeting with you."

Silence. Then, "Who?"

"Brian Overton, Rapid City PD." He felt like yelling into the phone. This shouldn't be so complicated. "He's on his way to you with Abigail and the files right now. He arranged for the SWAT team but then Sheriff Layton called it off…?" Maybe that would jog the man's memory.

"I'm sorry, Micah, but no one asked for a SWAT team." He paused, and when he spoke again, his next words fell like a bomb. "I've never spoken with Detective Overton."

TWELVE

"How are you holding up?" Detective Overton glanced at Abigail as the car curved around another bend in the road. They were heading west through the park, and soon they'd turn north to the interstate and Rapid City.

She slouched back against the seat, her entire body like jelly now that the immediate danger was over, even though the detective was pushing the car around these corners at a breakneck pace. He didn't have the siren on, but he'd come up fast enough behind a few tourists that they'd pulled over just to let the cruiser pass. His knuckles glowed white against tan skin from clutching the wheel so hard.

"I'm okay," she said, the answer almost automatic. What else could she say? Her son, her sister, Micah, herself... Any one of them could have died today. It was only by God's grace they'd walked out of that desert maze relatively unscathed. Watching Micah take that hit, and then lying there, injured… A place inside her chest had collapsed, and it threatened to do so again at the memory.

There was no denying she cared about him far more than she'd ever intended. And from the way he'd looked at her… Was there a chance it was mutual?

Did she want it to be?

She squirmed in the seat, as if readjusting her position could fix the mess inside her heart. Micah was nothing like Eric— he would have given his life for her today. And unlike what had happened with Eric, she knew the *real* Micah, not just a glossy magazine version she'd crafted in her own imagination. Life-and-death situations had a way of revealing people's hearts.

But relationships *always* came with risks. Was that something either of them was willing to face?

"Well, this will all be over soon." Brian flipped on his turn signal and turned north, accelerating as the road straightened. He kept glancing in his rearview mirror, almost like he expected someone to follow them.

And his posture was oddly rigid. Different from the relieved, I'm-so-glad-this-is-over way that she slumped in the passenger seat. Was it because he felt bad about what had happened with the sheriff?

"Micah said you have a baby daughter?" she asked, hoping to set him at ease.

He cleared his throat. "Um, yeah. Six months old. Her name is Hazel." He grew silent, and a muscle flickered in his jaw. They passed the ranger entrance station, and he pressed the accelerator hard enough that she jerked backward against her seat. Sweat dripped down the side of his forehead despite the blasting AC, and he swiped at his skin as he glanced in his rearview mirror again.

Something was definitely off. "When is the FBI agent expecting us?" she asked, fighting to keep her tone even. *Do you have to speed?*

"As soon as we can get there." The words came out raspy, even though there was no one else out here on the road. He glanced at the envelope sitting on her lap, his movements jerky. "You've got the files. What about the other envelope? With your husband's offshore accounts?"

She froze, her brain scrambling to process as every nerve went on high alert. Micah had agreed with her not to tell anyone about Eric's letter until they'd called the IRS. How had Brian heard about it? David? *He* would've known. He probably sat there next to Eric, advising him on the best ways to squirrel away his illegally earned fortune, acting like a friend until push came to shove. The mob would want that money back now if they could get their hands on it.

"How do you know about that?" She hated how strangled her voice sounded but clearing her throat didn't help. Not with these horrible thoughts running through her mind.

All along, every decision, every meeting, every new set of arrangements, had been filtered through Detective Overton. He was Micah's friend, and naturally Micah trusted him. But Abigail had trusted Eric for years too, and Eric had trusted David.

They'd thought Sheriff Layton was behind all the poor decisions and last-minute changes…but what if he wasn't the one who'd been bought off by the mob?

What if it was Brian Overton?

"Micah told me." His hands flexed on the steering wheel. He didn't look at her. "After you found the files."

Her stomach nose-dived into her knees. He was lying. She'd been with Micah for all those conversations, and he'd never once told Brian about those accounts. There was only one other way he could've found out.

Her palms grew slick, and she fought the urge to panic. "It was you all along, wasn't it? Not the sheriff. No wonder he looked so confused when Micah insisted you told him to post extra officers at Wall Drug. He never even knew about the SWAT team, did he?" She shook her head. "You didn't even contact the FBI field office, did you?"

Brian didn't take his eyes off the road, but his knuckles turned even whiter as he pushed the car faster. "Of course, I didn't. That would've been stupid."

"Where are we going?"

No answer, only the tightening of his jaw muscle. Into the desert then, somewhere he could kill her and no one would find her.

"I didn't want it to come to this," he said, blinking rapidly for a moment. "If David would've succeeded, I could've quietly packed up my family and left town. But no, David Blakely and his men failed."

"Now," he went on, "now there's no way out. I'm sorry it's come to this, Abigail, I truly am."

She shook her head, as if arguing could change reality. "I don't understand. Why would you help them? You're Micah's friend. He *trusted* you."

When he turned to look at her, the regret in

his eyes tore at her heart. "I didn't want to," he whispered, the words so low she could hardly hear them. "But after we rescued Owen from David the first time, they cornered me outside my house that night. Told me my wife and baby would be targeted next if I didn't make this case go away. They promised if I helped, if I made sure the files were never exposed and you didn't talk, they'd leave us alone." He took a hand from the wheel to pinch the bridge of his nose, though he kept up the car's relentless pace. "I know I shouldn't have done it, but I didn't see any other way out. Even now, there's only one way to keep Jules and Hazel safe."

"So you set up Layton to look like the bad guy." She pursed her lips. "And you must've fed them information about where to find me." That explained how they'd known she and Micah were meeting Eleanor at Wall Drug to swap Owen. And going to her house in Chicago. Disgust coiled in her gut, mingling with the pity she felt for him. After all, what Eric had done wasn't that much different, was it? David had lured him into working for the mob, and by the time he realized it, it was too late to get out without putting her and Owen in harm's way.

"I thought if I just set them in the right direction, I could keep out of it and it would all go away." His shoulders slumped. "But they wanted more and more, and before long, I was in too deep. Julie will never forgive me."

She sucked in a deep breath. Every fiber of her body screamed at her to panic, to unleash her terror and anger on him for everything she'd gone through, but deep down she knew God had words of life to offer him. Through her. "This doesn't have to be the end of the story, Brian. You can still stop this car, call Micah, and we'll go to the FBI office together. Explain what happened and set things right. You don't have to go through with whatever you're planning."

Tears streamed down his cheeks but he shook his head, his lips going tight. "It's too late. Don't you see that?" He fumbled in the center console and clicked on his phone, holding out a text message for her to see. A picture of a two-story home with a wide front porch. A woman sat in a rocker, holding a pink-clad baby and smiling. A line of words ran beneath the picture. Last chance to fix this or else.

"Look at the time stamp," he said.

10:17 a.m. Thirty minutes ago.

Her chest squeezed. "Call your department, Brian. They'll get officers to your house within minutes. You don't have to live in fear."

"And how has that worked out for you?" he demanded, rounding on her. "Has your son stayed safe? What about your husband?" He glanced in the rearview mirror and swore, punching the accelerator and jerking her forward again.

She turned around, her breath catching as she caught sight of an NPS SUV coming up fast on their tail. *Micah.* Hope fluttered beneath her ribs like a trapped butterfly.

"Please, Brian, slow down and pull over. Let us help." She pointed ahead at the interstate. The town of Wall was just on the other side, as evidenced by the increase in tourist traffic and the stoplight beneath the overpass. "RCPD can send someone to your house, and the sheriff's office is right up ahead."

"It's too late, Abigail." His tone had gone dead, and the cold lifelessness frightened her far more than his fear had. "I'm sorry."

They passed beneath the interstate, coming up on the traffic light on the far side, but Brian didn't slow the vehicle. Instead, he accelerated, despite the stopped car in front of them.

Abigail screamed as he cut around the car with a vicious swerve, narrowly avoiding a collision with an oncoming car. He jerked the wheel back to the right, overcorrecting. The car went careening toward the off-ramp for the westbound traffic.

No—

Her eyes went wide and a pit opened in her stomach. He hadn't overcorrected, he was heading the wrong direction onto I-90. On purpose.

To kill them.

"Stop!" she screamed, fumbling for the wheel, but he shoved her against the door and slammed the gas, pushing the car to fifty mph and climbing. Sixty. Seventy.

Up ahead, barreling down the long off-ramp at deadly speed, approached an eighteen-wheeler semi-truck. A loud honk blasted from the truck.

There was no time to think, only time to react. She pushed off from the door and lunged for the wheel, arm banging against the computer in the console, fingers clasping the smooth leather near the top. Brian's elbow dug sharply into her forearm, but she squeezed her hand tight and yanked the wheel to the right for all she was worth.

Brian cried out, hands flailing for the wheel, and Abigail's stomach shot up into her mouth as the cruiser barreled toward the right side of the off-ramp. The semi-truck flew by in a blur of white, the pitch of its horn changing as it passed. As soon as the car's front tires hit grass, it tipped precariously to one side, hanging in space for an eternity before momentum carried it side over side into a roll.

Abigail screamed, long and loud, and her throat burned. Images flashed before her eyes—Owen snuggled close to her side while they read a book, Eric's empty chair near the fire, the look on Micah's face when she'd knelt beside him hours before in the desert. If only she'd had the time to tell him how she felt. Life was too short to waste on being afraid.

Gentle warmth wrapped around her heart and the world went black.

"No!" Micah gripped the steering wheel and watched in horror as Brian's police cruiser hit the grass on the side of the off-ramp and flipped. Like a slow-motion action sequence in a film, the car windows shattered as the vehicle rolled side-over-side, finally shuddering to a stop.

He flipped on the SUV's lights and siren and cut up the shoulder on the right, driving onto the off-ramp past the eighteen-wheeler stopped at the light. A minivan coming down the ramp slowed, no doubt gawking at the flipped cop car, and gave Micah's vehicle a wide berth as he drove up the ramp on the shoulder.

Though it cost an extra thirty seconds, as soon as he parked, he grabbed the radio and called the Pennington County dispatcher. The sheriff's office would get someone over here within minutes.

Along with an ambulance.

The blood throbbed in his temples as he climbed out of the car and raced for the wreck. Brian's car had settled upside-down in the grass halfway between the ramp and the interstate, where traffic whizzed past. Thankfully the cruiser's frame was built to withstand a rollover, so the top hadn't completely crushed in.

He flung himself to the ground on the passenger side, crawling up to the broken window. Abigail and Brian were both still buckled in their seats, but neither moved. Blood dripped from a wound on Abigail's forehead, running ruby-red into her hairline.

A band tightened around his chest, cinching so tight he could hardly breathe. *Please, God.* The prayer ripped out of his soul more in shape than in words.

"Abigail?" He reached inside and touched

her cheek. *Warm.* She'd braced her arms across her chest, and one hand dangled near her chin. "Abigail, can you hear me?"

The fingers moved, and he took them in his hand, squeezing gently. "Hey, you still with me?"

Her eyes flickered open, wide and unfocused until her green gaze landed on him. Still alive. Relief crashed through him in a wave so intense he might melt into the grass.

"Micah?" her voice was grainy and thick, like her brain didn't want to cooperate. Not surprising, after a wreck like this. But the rest of her appeared uninjured. "Why are you upside down?"

His lips twitched as gratitude ballooned in his chest. "Let's get you out of here, okay? Can you put your hands up to brace yourself?" Carefully he cleared away fragments of safety glass to give her space.

She pulled both arms away from her chest, reaching down to touch the roof of the car beneath her.

"I'm going to unbuckle you, okay?"

"I'm ready."

He scooched forward until his shoulder butted against the door frame, then leaned inside and reached upward to press the button. Her soft breath caressed his cheek. The seat belt released, and she grunted with the strain of supporting herself. Micah pulled back and placed his hands on her shoulders, helping ease her downward and out of the shattered window, until he was cradling her in his arms.

She smiled up at him, the freckles dancing on her nose, and he was certain she'd never looked more beautiful.

"Are you all right? Can you feel your toes? Hands?" The words came out in a hoarse whisper as he scanned her from head to toe. Not far away, sirens cut through the whizzing of the nearby interstate traffic.

She nodded, her eyes filling with tears. As she blinked, they trickled out onto her cheeks, making his heart clench. "I'm okay. God protected me."

Yes, He had. He'd protected them all today. Even Brian, who groaned from inside the vehicle. *Thank You.*

"He gave me another chance," she went on. "Because I have to tell you something."

"I have to tell you something too."

Her green eyes went wide. "You do?"

"Yeah." The swelling inside his chest burned his esophagus, making his eyes water. How was it possible to hold this many feelings for another person? "Abigail Fox, I'm in love with you. I didn't plan for it to happen."

He blinked the moisture away, glancing up as two police cars screeched to a halt on the off-ramp nearby. "And I sure didn't plan to tell you right here."

She laughed, soft and promising and beautiful. "I don't mind. Because—" her throat bobbed "—I love you too. I didn't think it was possible to care this much about someone else, to feel so much like you belong together. I know there're no guarantees about the future or what God will allow to happen, but you're worth the risk, Micah Ellis."

He leaned down, kissing the tears staining her cheeks. Then her lips, soft and warm. Like finding the other half of himself he'd been missing all these years.

"Thank you for protecting me and Owen," she whispered as he pulled back.

He smiled, happiness radiating all the way down to his toes. "There's no one I'd rather protect."

Nearby someone cleared their throat, and Micah glanced over his shoulder to see Sheriff Layton standing close by. On the other side of the car, two officers worked to extract a semiconscious Brian Overton from the driver's side.

Micah touched his forehead in salute. "Sheriff."

"Ranger Ellis, I see Ms. Fox is in good hands."

Heat flared up his neck, but there was no stopping the huge grin that spread across his face. "Just making sure she's all right."

"I am now." Her green gaze didn't leave his face.

There'd be work to do—the case to resolve, feelings to sort out around Brian's betrayal, hard decisions to make—but for right now, in this moment, he held the woman he loved close in his arms and thanked God for His endless, unfathomable goodness and grace.

EPILOGUE

Ten months later

"Mr. Micah! Mr. Micah! Is it time?"

Micah finished adjusting his tie and turned around to swoop up the little boy as he darted up to his legs.

"Micah Ellis, you're going to crumple his suit. What will Abigail say?" Eleanor shook her head at him from the doorway.

"She's going to say how handsome we both look anyway." He winked at Owen, hugged him tightly, and then set him back down.

Nearby, Nick Langston laughed and guided Owen back to his aunt. "You better get going, young man. You have a big job. If you don't get those rings down the aisle, the wedding won't happen."

His little eyes went wide. "Really?"

Micah scowled at the chief ranger, who was practically unrecognizable decked out in a tuxedo instead of an NPS uniform, and knelt in front of Owen. "He's kidding. If you think there's anything that could stop me from marrying your mom, then you should know I love you and her more than anything else in the world."

A grin split the little boy's face. "I love you too, Mr. Micah!" He skipped out of the room with Abigail's sister, who had a hand pressed to her heart as she blinked back tears.

As Micah followed Nick, his best man, out into the Rapid City church's sanctuary, he couldn't help but marvel at God's hand on his life. After all the heartache he'd endured, he'd thought it was up to him to guard his heart. But God had brought this amazing woman into his life—one who was also struggling with pain and loss—and He'd shown them both how much they needed each other. How even though their human minds could never grasp His plans, He was in control.

They'd made it through the trial, both taking the stand to testify against David Blakely and the other mob members who'd helped him. Eric's files had stood up against the court's scrutiny, allowing the prosecutor to pin the *don* and take down an entire branch of the Chicago mafia. And the IRS had allowed Abigail to keep the money, though she'd donated most of it to a Chicago women's shelter. When the case was over and he'd asked her to marry him, she hadn't hesitated in saying yes. Between packing up and selling her house in Chicago, planning the wedding, and prepping for their move to Estes Park for his new assignment at Rocky Mountain National Park, the last few months had passed in a whirlwind.

But finally they'd reached today, where Micah stood in the front of the church he'd attended these past three years, with his father in the front row and friends gathered to watch. Brian Overton's absence made his heart twinge, but he'd be lifting the former detective and his family up in prayer regularly, asking God to use this tragedy in his life to lead him to the Lord. His wife had stuck with him, even though he'd be serving a lengthy jail term, and Micah truly wished the best for them.

The soft music the pianist had been playing suddenly shifted to the bridal processional, and all thoughts vanished out of Micah's mind as his gaze snapped to the back of the sanctuary. Eleanor came first, beautiful in a flowing maid of honor dress and leading Owen by the hand. The little boy wore a huge grin, nearly skipping down the aisle, and he waggled the white pillow with the two gold rings tied to it as soon as he realized Micah was watching him.

Then the rest of the world vanished and Micah saw nothing else but Abigail. She'd chosen a simple satin and lace gown, with the veil tucked underneath her upswept auburn hair in the back rather than covering her face. She held her father's arm as he escorted her up the aisle, until finally the moment came where Micah took her small hands in his, and they offered their promises for a lifetime of love and commitment.

When the "I do's" were over and the rings had been exchanged, he leaned in to kiss her in front of God and their family and friends.

"Thank you," she whispered against his cheek. "For choosing me."

He pulled back to look at her face. The audience broke into applause, but he barely noticed them. A man could get lost in those deep green eyes. "Thank *you* for being brave enough to say yes. I can't imagine my life without you." He grinned, waving at Owen, who sat in the front row with Abigail's mother. "Both of you."

Owen broke loose from his grandmother and dashed up the steps until he clung to both their legs. Micah laughed, scooping the boy up, and pulled both him and Abigail into an embrace.

Their eyes met over the top of Owen's head. Laughter danced in Abigail's gaze, making his heart feel like it might split its seams and burst with happiness. God had made them a family, and they'd only experienced the beginning of His blessings to come.

* * * * *

Dear Reader,

Thank you so much for joining me and Micah, Abigail and Owen on their adventure in South Dakota's Badlands. My family was able to visit this rugged and scenic part of the country several years ago on a camping trip. One of my kids' favorite things about the national park was that they were allowed to hike and climb wherever they liked. We also visited Wall Drug and the Minuteman Missile sites. While my husband took a tour of the Launch Facility, my young kids entertained themselves by watching a caterpillar crawl across the sign, just like Owen does in the book. I didn't let them take it home, either.

Both Abigail and Micah have endured their share of painful circumstances in the past, leading them to question whether God truly cares about them on a personal level. It's easy to have faith when times are good, but a whole lot harder during trials. When challenging times hit in my life, I find the best answer at the cross, where Jesus paid the ultimate price to show His boundless love for us. Not only can we experience His peace and comfort now, but we look forward to the day when all these trials and difficulties will fade away in His glorious presence. Now that's a reason to have hope!

I love hearing from readers, so feel free to get in touch on my Facebook author page (@authorkellievanhorn) or through my website www.kellievanhorn.com, where you can also sign up for my author newsletter.

Warmly,
Kellie VanHorn